The Peaks of Ecstasy

The Private Chapel was small but beautifully decorated, and the altar was covered with flowers.

Lord Roydon stood in front of the altar, waiting for his Bride.

The Viceroy gave her away in the conventional fashion.

The Chaplain read the Service with the same sincerity as the Vicar had done in the village of Little Wick.

But Geta knew, as she listened, that something was missing.

It was love.

When Lord Roydon placed the wedding-ring on her finger Geta could not help remembering that he was called "The Icicle."

It flashed through her mind that perhaps he would never love her . . .

A Camfield Novel of Love
by Barbara Cartland

"Barbara Cartland's novels are all distinguished by their intelligence, good sense, and good nature. . . ."

—ROMANTIC TIMES

"Who could give better advice on how to keep your romance going strong than the world's most famous romance novelist, Barbara Cartland?"

—THE STAR

Camfield Place,
Hatfield
Hertfordshire,
England

Dearest Reader,

Camfield Novels of Love mark a very exciting era of my books with Jove. They have already published nearly two hundred of my titles since they became my first publisher in America, and now all my original paperback romances in the future will be published exclusively by them.

As you already know, Camfield Place in Hertfordshire is my home, which originally existed in 1275, but was rebuilt in 1867 by the grandfather of Beatrix Potter.

It was here in this lovely house, with the best view in the county, that she wrote *The Tale of Peter Rabbit*. Mr. McGregor's garden is exactly as she described it. The door in the wall that the fat little rabbit could not squeeze underneath and the goldfish pool where the white cat sat twitching its tail are still there.

I had Camfield Place blessed when I came here in 1950 and was so happy with my husband until he died, and now with my children and grandchildren, that I know the atmosphere is filled with love and we have all been very lucky.

It is easy here to write of love and I know you will enjoy the Camfield Novels of Love. Their plots are definitely exciting and the covers very romantic. They come to you, like all my books, with love.

Bless you,

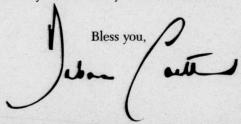

CAMFIELD NOVELS OF LOVE

by Barbara Cartland

A NEW CAMFIELD NOVEL OF LOVE BY

BARBARA CARTLAND

The Peaks of Ecstasy

JOVE BOOKS, NEW YORK

THE PEAKS OF ECSTASY

A Jove Book / published by arrangement with
the author

PRINTING HISTORY
Jove edition / April 1993

ISBN: 0-515-11085-X

Jove Books are published by The Berkley Publishing Group,
200 Madison Avenue, New York, New York 10016.
The name "JOVE" and the "J" logo
are trademarks belonging to Jove Publications, Inc.

PRINTED IN THE UNITED STATES OF AMERICA

10 9 8 7 6 5 4 3 2 1

Author's Note

ANYONE who goes to India cannot help but be tremendously impressed by what are now called "The Palaces of the Raj."

Government House in Calcutta was, even when it was first built, considered the finest Governor's Palace in the world.

In 1798 the young Irish peer, Richard Wellesley, Earl of Mornington, arrived as Governor General. He brought with him carriages, stores, and baggage valued at 2,000 pounds.

Less than a month after his arrival the Earl decided the Government House was "unworthy of his station." Building began in 1799 while the Earl was engaged in a war against Tipu Sultan.

He won, and was created Marquess Wellesley as a reward for his success.

The Palace rising up in Calcutta was a symbol of the growth of British power. It was finished in four years and cost 63,291 pounds.

It was then, as I think it is now, the finest building in the whole of the East.

When I first saw it I was overcome at how magnificent it was. This was not surprising, as it was copied from the Derbyshire Mansion, Kedleston Hall, which I have used in so many of my novels, as it was the finest example of the work of the Brothers Adam.

The arrangements, however, for the kitchen quarters were extraordinary, as the kitchen was not just outside the house, but outside the grounds in one of the narrow and inevitably squalid streets that flanked the northern approach.

Lady Dufferin's comments soon after her husband's arrival as Viceroy was:

"The kitchen is somewhere in Calcutta, but not in this house."

The food had to travel 200 yards in *dhoolies*, or boxes on poles. The Private Secretary's office was relegated to neighbouring premises.

It was not until the opening years of the present century that Lord Curzon cleared these streets and erected ranges of offices on their site.

Lord Curzon was the great modernizer of Government House. He replaced the old green-painted wooden tubs with fixed baths though they had, in fact, had hot and cold running water for the past twenty years.

The house had been lit with gas as far back as 1857, but in Lord Curzon's time it was first lit by electricity. He introduced electric lifts and electric fans, while keeping the old hand *punkahs* in the Marble Hall and the other state apartments, preferring, he said: "their measured sweep" to what he called "the hideous anachronism of the revolving blades."

The Peaks of Ecstasy

chapter one

1899

WALKING back home after her Mother's Funeral
with her two sisters, Geta was wondering what
would happen to them in the future.

They had lived in the beautiful Queen Anne
house all their lives.

Her Father had bought it when he married.

Now they learnt that for some strange reason,
years ago he had left it, on his wife's death, to a
Cousin who was very keen on Architecture.

"How could Papa have done such a thing?"
Geta had asked angrily.

It had been a shock when their Mother's Solici-
tor had told them after she died that they would
have to leave.

"Papa was much richer in those days," Linette
explained. "In fact, he was making a lot of money from his books, and besides, he had invest-
ments which were paying good dividends."

"What happened to them?" Madeline asked
plaintively.

"Papa's last book was never published, and the dividends have mostly disappeared."

It was a gloomy conversation.

Then their anxiety had to be put aside while they made arrangements for the Funeral.

Their Mother, Lady Naunton, had been very popular.

They knew everybody in the County would want to pay tribute to her.

But they had in that part of Worcestershire not many near neighbours.

Therefore it was the village folk they had to think of first.

Because Lady Naunton had been kind, understanding, and compassionate, they all loved her.

The villagers of their own village, Little Wick, were not the only people whom she had helped.

"Yer Mother were like an Angel a-comin' down from Heaven to 'elp us," the villagers from all around them used to say.

If they were in trouble with their families, their health, or a dozen other problems, they always turned up at the back-door, saying:

"Can Oi see 'er Ladyship?"

Geta found it hard to believe that her Mother was really dead.

She had been indisposed after Christmas with a bad cold and complained of having a sore throat.

She stayed in the house, which for her was unusual.

But they had not realised she was really ill.

A week ago she was unable to leave her bed.

Then she died.

"How can it be true?" Geta cried.

The Doctor had told them gently that their Mother had passed away peacefully in her sleep.

"It is the way most people would wish to die," Dr. Graham said.

He was very fond of the girls.

He had brought all of them into the world.

But he was now an elderly man and found it difficult to know how to comfort these three beautiful young creatures.

They were suddenly bereft, not only of their Mother, but also of their home.

"What shall we do? What shall we ... do?" Geta asked herself as they walked away from the grave.

There was a mass of flowers heaped over it once the Undertakers had finished covering it with soil.

There were several large, important-looking wreaths from the County people.

The villagers, however, had made their own simple contributions.

There were little bunches of violets and daffo-dils which were just showing gold in the cottage gardens.

They were all expressions of love.

As the coffin was lowered into the grave, there was not a dry eye amongst those standing around it.

'Life can never be the same again without Mama,' Geta thought despairingly.

Their house was only a short walk from the Church.

As they came in sight of the beautiful Queen Anne building, Geta wanted to cry.

It was so unfair that they had lost not only their Mother, but also their home.

"How could Papa have done anything so foolish?" she asked.

Sir Reginald Naunton had been dead for three years and could not defend his action.

'I suppose, if the truth were known,' Geta thought, 'he would have expected us to be married before Mama died.'

They had not invited the people who had attended the Funeral back to the house.

It would have been an expense they could not afford.

As the Service had been arranged for two-thirty in the afternoon, to do so was quite unnecessary.

Linette, who was always practical, said firmly:

"No! It would cost us all the money we have, and what would be the point of that?"

As they walked into the panelled Hall, Geta looked round her.

Everything in it was very precious.

It would all remain in her memory forever.

The big Grandfather clock, the beautiful Queen Anne table which had always been a part of the house.

The mirrors which her Father had found in a small antique shop in Bath.

The chairs he had bought at a sale where no-one knew their history.

The three girls went into the Drawing-Room.

Their Mother had made it very elegant when she had first married.

It had become rather shabby over the years, but it was still lovely and furnished in perfect good taste.

Good taste was also inbred in her Father, and this was what had made the first books he wrote such a success.

They were on antiques, first on those in England, then after he was married on those in other countries.

Linette belonged to his French Period.

He had become obsessed with the period of Louis XIV.

The building of the Palace at Versailles had thrilled him.

He described the tapestries, the furniture, and the pictures which were all part of the "Sun King's" reign.

He wrote well, amusingly, and with an undeniable knowledge not given to many people.

His books had therefore sold a great number of copies and won him a National reputation.

Linette, when she was born, had been given a French name.

Almost as if she responded to pre-natal influence, she had black hair and might in fact have come from France.

Her sister Madeline was born two years later.

She belonged to her Father's Hebrew period.

He had visited Jerusalem and was thrilled with all he'd found there.

He had journeyed with their Mother to Damascus and to the site where it was believed Troy had once stood.

He found new things to write about them and ancient legends to tell, which made his new book again a best-seller.

They had come home in order that he might write it.

Madeline was born and of course given a Hebrew name.

Geta was the next, but her period was rather different from that of her sisters'.

Sir Reginald had become interested in the Latin language and how its use had spread over western Europe.

Geta's name meant in Latin "Divine Power."

Lady Naunton had been delighted when her husband had chosen it for their daughter.

However, the new book was not such a success as the previous ones had been.

It was indeed more erudite, more scholarly.

But while it was acclaimed as a great piece of writing, the sales were not very large.

It was after Geta was born that Sir Reginald had begun to write another book on a subject which he found absorbing.

It took a very long time.

It was about the development of the products of every country in the world in relation to the characteristic way of thinking and feeling in each country.

Every time it seemed he was getting to the end of it, he discovered a new country, one which he had not previously mentioned.

That meant more research, another Chapter, and a further delay before it went to the Publishers.

Spread over the years, it ran into six volumes.

He had only just finished the last one when he died.

The sad thing was that after so much endeavour, people had forgotten Sir Reginald's earlier successes.

The Publishers were not eager to print so many volumes by an Author who had been forgotten by his public after so long.

When the girls received the third refusal, Geta asked:

"How can Papa have been so stupid as to go on writing all those years about something that nobody wanted to read?"

"It is what he enjoyed," Linette replied, "and you know Mama encouraged him to go on simply because she wanted him to be happy."

Her Mother had adored her husband.

She had been supremely happy with him whether they were sitting quietly in Worcestershire or travelling to various parts of the world.

Sir Reginald had married her when he was nearly forty.

He had therefore not been so keen later to make the adventurous journeys which they had made when they first married.

"I have what I want to say in my mind," he remarked, "and I can always go to the British Museum in London for anything else I need to know."

Lady Naunton had been perfectly happy so long as she was with him.

The girls, therefore, grew up in the quietness of the countryside.

They had their horses to ride and were content to be with themselves.

One thing her Father insisted upon was that they should be well-educated.

He had an absolute genius for discovering retired School-Masters.

"They," he said, "are far better qualified to teach you than a young Governess."

He also discovered Musicians who were longing to impart their knowledge of music to intelligent pupils.

There were also a number of foreigners available who spoke the languages Sir Reginald wanted his daughters to learn.

They were all very proficient in French.

They had an Italian shop-owner with whom they spoke Italian.

After several other teachers whom he dismissed after a few months, their Father himself taught them his beloved Latin.

He told them it was the foundation for most European languages.

Sir Reginald's Library was filled with every sort of book on every possible subject.

The girls, therefore, were exceedingly well-read.

He felt sad only that he did not have a son to carry on the work that he was doing.

"Women do not have the same interest that I have in the development of furniture, painting and sculpture or fabrics," he said to his wife.

"I know, darling, but your daughters are all very beautiful, and you cannot expect them also to be as brilliant at writing as you are."

Sir Reginald had laughed.

But it was something he deeply regretted.

He therefore tried to make up for his daughters' deficiencies in not being sons.

'We were very, very happy,' Geta thought as she entered the Drawing-Room.

Then she heard Linette give an exclamation of surprise.

"What is it?" Madeline asked.

"There is a letter for Mama. The Postman must have brought it when we were at the Church."

"I wonder who it is from?" Geta said. "You had better open it."

"I am going to," Linette said. "Actually it comes from India."

"From India?" Madeline exclaimed. "Who could be writing to Mama from India?"

Her sister walked across the room to sit down in a comfortable armchair.

She did not answer, but opened the envelope carefully.

Then, as she took out the letter and looked at the signature, she said:

"It is from Cousin Silvius."

"We have not heard from him for years," Madeline said. "I wonder why he is writing to Mama now."

"As far as I remember," Linette replied, "he did not send her a card at Christmas, and it is a long time since I heard her mention him."

Geta was re-arranging some flowers.

They had been in bud when she had first brought them in from the garden.

Now, because they had bloomed, they looked congested in the vase in which she had put them.

"Shall I read it aloud?" Linette asked. "It cannot be one of condolence, as there is no way he could have known that Mama has died."

"Yes, read it," Madeline agreed.

Linette did so in her soft, very attractive voice:

"Dear Cousin Elizabeth,

You may be surprised to hear from me, and I feel guilty at having left it so long, but a great number of things have happened. You may not be aware that I have been honoured by Her Majesty the Queen by being given a Peerage . . ."

"Good Heavens," Madeline exclaimed, "that is very smart!"

Linette went on:

"I have chosen to keep my own name, but I am now Lord Roydon of Wick. I tried to think of some particular part of England that is of special importance in my life, but as you know, my parents' house was burnt down some years ago and the only house of any distinction left in the family is your own.

I therefore feel certain that you will not mind my having taken it as part of my title . . ."

"It seems to me," Madeline said, "that it is a great pity Papa did not leave the house to him instead of that tiresome Cousin Simon, who has never bothered with us in any way and wrote to say he could not come to Mama's Funeral because he was going abroad, and did not even send a wreath!"

"I thought that was disgraceful," Linette agreed, "and do you remember the postscript he added:

" 'When I return from Spain, I will come to see you about the house.' "

Geta thought her sister was right in thinking that her Cousin Simon was abominable.

She was only wondering what they could take away from the house when they had to leave.

Anything of course that her Father had bought for the house after he had bequeathed it to their Cousin could be theirs.

Geta, however, had the uncomfortable feeling that in fact included very few of the larger pieces of furniture.

Her Father had completed the house exactly as he wanted it before he made his Will.

"Go on with the letter," Madeline prompted her sister.

"There is a lot more here," Linette replied, turning over a page. "I cannot think why he has so much to say."

Then she read:

"What I am really writing to you about, and I feel sure you will help me, is that I need a wife. I have been told in confidence by the Vice-

11

roy that as soon as I have a wife, I am to be offered a Governorship out here, which I very much want.

Unfortunately I find the Englishwomen in India who would accept the position with pleasure would not be at all the type of wife I require and in fact in many ways shock me by their behaviour.

I am therefore suggesting, Cousin Elizabeth, that I should marry one of your daughters. I know how well they have been brought up and how intelligent they both are, and that is exactly what I require in the very difficult job I will have to do out here.

It is one of great responsibility and importance to the Empire.

As I wish to have everything settled as soon as possible, I should be grateful if you would cable me as to which of your daughters, whom I met some years ago, will honour me by becoming my wife.

I enclose the address of the Manager of the Thomas Cook Branch in Mayfair, who has in the past always served me well on my journeys to and from India.

He will see to it that your daughter has the best accommodation on a P. & O. Liner sailing to Bombay and will also, I know, find her a chaperon amongst the passengers.

I have already cabled him that I will be responsible for any expenses that are incurred, and he will be waiting for you to get in touch with him.

I can only promise you that I will do my best

*to make your daughter happy. I am confident
that as your and Cousin Reginald's child, she
will know how to live up to my position with
dignity and intelligence.*

> *I remain,*
> *Yours very sincerely,*
> *Silvius Roydon."*

As Linette finished reading the letter, both her
sisters gasped.

"I have never heard of such a thing!" Madeline
exclaimed. "I suppose because he is now a Lord
he thinks we are going to jump over the moon
with excitement at the prospect of having him
as a husband."

"I find it most presumptuous of him!" Linette
agreed. "But as it happens, I am not in the con-
test because though I have not told you two
before, I am going to marry Henry Preston."

"Oh, Linette!" Madeline cried. "Why did you
not tell us?"

"I was just going to when Mama died, and
it would have been heartless when we had the
Funeral to think about. But Henry has insisted
that he is not going to wait for the conventional
year of mourning before we marry, with me
looking like a black crow. We are going to be
married in a week's time, and go immediately
abroad."

"It is the most exciting thing I have ever
heard!" Madeline exclaimed.

Geta ran across the room to kiss her sister.

"I like Henry Preston," she said, "and he is
very, very rich!"

"Yes, he is," Linette replied, "and I do wish Mama could have known that I am to marry him."

They all knew their Mother had often said piteously that she wished there were more young men in the neighbourhood.

It worried her how they were ever to meet and marry someone of the right age.

It was just by chance that Linette had had the opportunity of riding a spirited horse belonging to a local Farmer.

His son, who usually rode it, had injured his leg.

The son was worrying because *Firebrand*, as the horse was called, was not getting sufficient exercise.

Linette had been riding one of her Father's horses which was getting old when she had met Farmer Jackson.

"Oi was wondering, Miss Linette," he said, "if you'd do me a great favour."

Linette smiled at him.

"Of course I will," she replied. "And Mama was asking only yesterday about your son's leg and hoping it was getting better."

"It's healing slowly," the Farmer replied, "but me boy's worrying himself silly over *Firebrand*. As ye knows, Miss Linette, 'e be a spirited horse an' needs a lot o' exercise, but th' lads as work for Oi be too frightened to mount 'im."

Linette's eyes sparkled.

"I would love to ride *Firebrand*," she said. "I will come up this afternoon and gallop some of the mischief out of him."

"That be real kind o' ye," the Farmer said, "an' Bill 'll be ever so grateful."

Linette was an excellent rider, like her sisters.

She was only too thrilled to have the chance of riding a horse that she longed to own.

It had been difficult enough since her Father's death to keep the two old horses they possessed.

They also drew the carriage which her Mother used when she went out.

To ride *Firebrand*, who was very difficult to hold, was very exciting.

She therefore took him even farther than she had intended.

Then she made him jump a high fence.

On the other side of it she saw a young man.

He was also riding a well-bred horse and was looking at her in astonishment.

She realised she was trespassing, and as she pulled in *Firebrand*, she said:

"I am sorry if I am on your land, but I could not resist that fence and neither could *Firebrand*."

"Is that the name of your horse?" the young man asked.

"I wish he *were* my horse!" Linette replied. "I am doing the owner a kindness in riding him, but I can assure you it is something which is very kind for me!"

The young man laughed, and that was the beginning.

It was impossible for anyone not to realise how lovely Linette was.

With her cheeks flushed, her eyes shining, and riding the large black stallion, she looked, as

Henry told her later, like Diana the Huntress.

After that, whenever Linette exercised *Fire-brand* she met Henry Preston.

"You cannot have a grand wedding," Madeline said, "but it will be very exciting for you to go abroad."

"Henry is taking me to Paris to buy my trousseau," Linette said.

Both girls gave a cry of delight.

"A French trousseau! Oh, Linette, how lucky you are!"

"Very lucky," Linette agreed, "but I would marry Henry if he had not a penny. However, it does make it easier that he is rich."

"Of course it does," Geta said, "and you will look very beautiful in the lovely French gowns which we have talked about but never have been able to afford."

"I think Papa would be very pleased," Linette said softly.

"Of course he would," Geta agreed.

There was silence, and both she and Linette looked at Madeline.

"If you are thinking of me going out to India to marry Cousin Silvius, you can think again!" Madeline said. "If Linette had her secret, I had mine."

"A secret?" Linette exclaimed. "What is it?"

"I did not tell you because Mama was ill, but I have been meeting a young man whom I found sketching the house one day. He said he thought it was the most beautiful building he had ever seen."

"A young man!" Linette exclaimed. "But who

16

is he? What do you know about him?"

"I did not know anything at first," Madeline replied, "but when you were out and Mama was asleep upstairs, I showed him the rooms downstairs because he was so interested. He knows a great deal about houses and furniture, which I know would have pleased Papa."

"Who is he?" Linette insisted.

"He told me at first just that his name was Sheldon. But when I had seen him two or three times I found he was actually a Baronet."

Both her sisters gasped.

"A Baronet? And has he asked you to marry him?" Geta questioned.

Madeline looked down a little shyly before she said:

"Not yet, but I am sure he will. I think he was afraid of 'rushing his fences,' so to speak, when Mama was ill and we are so upset."

"And you really think he intends to ask you?" Linette enquired.

"I know he will," Madeline answered. "And you may think it strange because you do not know him, but I am very much in love."

Geta sat down in one of the armchairs.

"I think you two are absolutely horrible," she said, "to have kept these secrets from me! You know I would have been so excited for you both, and you never said a word!"

Linette smiled at her.

"You must forgive us," she said, "but because it was so exciting and because I was so happy, I wanted to keep it all to myself just for a little while."

"I felt the same," Madeline said, "and, of course, when James did ask me to be his wife, I was going to tell you at once."

She looked at Linette a little reproachfully.

It was what she thought she should have done.

"Well, we can write and tell Cousin Silvius that neither of us is available," Linette said, "and he will have to look elsewhere for a wife."

"We had better cable him," Madeline said practically, "because he is in a hurry."

"I will do that," Linette answered, "and between ourselves, I am delighted that after his sending Mama such an extraordinary letter, we can tell him that we cannot accede to his request."

"I will marry him," Geta said quietly.

Both her sisters turned to look at her in astonishment.

"*You* will marry him?" Linette cried. "But you have never seen him. When he came here five years ago, he dropped in unexpectedly, and I remember you were having lessons with the School-Master."

Geta did not speak, and Madeline remarked:

"You were only twelve or thirteen at the time, so he obviously does not realise that you even exist."

"I know that," Geta said, "but you are both going to be married very soon . . . and what do you suggest I should do?"

"I have thought of that," Linette said quickly, "and Henry is quite certain that he will be able to find you someone near us with whom you can live."

She spoke a little diffidently, and Geta said:

"That means, I suppose, as a companion to some crotchety old lady, or else as a Nursery Governess to somebody's children!"

"I am sure it will be something better than that, Darling," Linette answered, "and I really have thought about you."

She smiled at her sister before she continued:

"But I know you will understand that when we first marry I shall want to be alone with Henry, and however tactful you were, it could be a little difficult to have my sister with me."

"I have no intention of living where I am not wanted!" Geta said. "And although I did not know you were marrying anybody, it is exactly what I would expect you to say in the circumstances."

"But . . . you cannot go off to India and marry a man you have never even seen!" Linette said. "It is a ghastly idea!"

"He cannot be as awful as all that if he is a Cousin of Mama's," Geta argued. "She always boasted about how important and well-bred the Roydons are and, quite frankly, I think she would be pleased."

"I think she would be horrified!" Madeline said. "She fell in love with Papa as soon as she saw him, and he with her. She would never have married a man to whom she had never even spoken!"

"If it is a question of earning my living with a lot of strangers, or being the wife of a stranger," Geta said, "I would choose the latter."

There was silence.

Then Linette said:

"I think, Dearest, because we love you, I should tell you a little about Cousin Silvius."

"What about him?" Geta asked. "He sounds clever."

"Oh, he is clever all right," Linette said, "but he is said to be a very difficult person. I think, having read his letter, it is exactly like him to want a wife sent out to India as if she were a package, rather than coming himself to look for one!"

There was silence again.

Then Madeline said:

"Thinking back, and it was all those years ago since he came here, I thought he was very good-looking."

"Oh, he is that!" Linette agreed. "But Mama told me after he had gone that he has always been the most difficult member of her family, and they were all in fact rather frightened of him."

"Why should they be frightened of him?" Geta asked.

"I can understand his being the right sort of person to be a Governor," Linette remarked. "He would love giving orders and enjoy all the pomp and ceremony. Henry would hate that sort of life!"

Her sisters did not say anything, and she went on:

"According to Mama, Cousin Silvius was brought up thinking, because he was an only child, that he was very important and that no-one was his equal."

"I remember his seeming somewhat self-assertive," Madeline said, "and I thought it rude of him to argue with Papa."

"I thought the same," Linette agreed, "and he had a cold, supercilious air about him which made me feel I was very young and very stupid."

Madeline laughed.

"Nobody, Dearest, could call you stupid! And Papa would have snapped his head off if Cousin Silvius had ventured to make such a remark."

"Oh, he did not discuss me or you," Linette replied. "He just made it obvious that he had no time for young girls by talking almost exclusively to Papa and only occasionally throwing a few words to me like scraps to a dog."

Madeline laughed.

"I remember now—that is exactly what he was like!"

Geta got up from the chair to walk to the window.

Linette looked after her with a worried look on her face.

"We are being rather unkind," she said, "but, Dearest Geta, it is because I love you that I do not want you to make a mistake."

She paused a moment and then continued:

"After all, marriage is for ever, and suppose you hate Cousin Silvius the moment you arrive in India? There will then be nothing you can do about it."

"I could always run away," Geta replied. "But at least I shall have seen India!"

"But you do not understand," Linette insisted as if she were a child. "Once he knows you are on your way out, he will arrange your marriage and you will very likely find yourself being taken up the aisle as soon as you step off the ship!"

"Then I will have to say I am suffering from travel sickness and he will have to wait a day or two until I have recovered."

Geta spoke in a light tone, which made Madeline say:

"Now, listen, Darling, you are making a joke of the whole thing, and marriage is not a joke. Linette is right—of course you cannot go out to India and marry Cousin Silvius just because he wants a wife."

She stopped speaking a moment and then went on sternly:

"I think the whole thing is insulting, and the sooner we tell him to look elsewhere, the better!"

"I am not insulted," Geta contradicted, "simply because I have been worrying ever since Mama died what would happen to us. Have you forgotten that as soon as Cousin Simon comes back from Spain he will take over this house and everything in it?"

She looked at her sisters and then continued:

"We shall own practically nothing except the clothes we stand up in. And while you two have rich husbands to look after you, I have no-one."

"I have already said that Henry and I will do our best to find you somewhere happy to live."

"Doing what?" Geta asked.

There was no answer to this, and as Linette did not reply, Geta said:

"I have always wanted to go to India. If nothing else, it will be an exciting adventure to see the country."

"But you will have Cousin Silvius waiting for you," Madeline said, "and you must be sensible about this. It will be very difficult to tell him after he has paid your fare that you have no wish to marry him."

"If the occasion arises, I will find some way of making him understand," Geta said. "I was thinking as the three of us left the Church that at least we were all in the same boat. But you have both been clever enough to escape from what we all know is an unpleasant and difficult situation."

She moved to stand in front of the mantelpiece, facing her sisters, and said:

"Do you realise that we have practically no money between us? While you two may be very generous to me, that will hardly pay for a roof over my head, even if it is nothing but a cottage."

"But . . . you cannot live alone!" Linette said quickly.

"Then we get back to the fact that I shall have to work for my living for somebody who does not want me and is only obliging Henry Preston or perhaps Sir James Sheldon."

"I know James will be only too pleased to help you," Madeline said, "and I think you are being very stupid."

"I think I am being very practical!" Geta

answered. "A drowning man does not argue about who throws him a lifebelt when he is sinking."

Linette folded the letter and replaced it in the envelope.

"Very well, Darling," she sighed, "you must do what you want to do, but I am not going to pretend that I am not terribly worried about your marrying Cousin Silvius. I have not yet told you, but he is known amongst some of Mama's relations as 'The Icicle' and others refer to him as 'The Rock.' "

Geta laughed.

"Then it is a challenge," she said, "as to whether I can 'melt the icicle' or 'dent the rock.' And it is quite apparent that neither of you are betting on me!"

Linette rose to her feet.

"You are making a joke of the whole thing," she protested. "Quite frankly, I am very worried . . . and I know Mama would be too . . . if she were alive."

Her voice broke when she spoke of her Mother, and she went quickly from the room.

Madeline put out her hand towards her sister.

"You are only just eighteen, Geta," she said, "and you know very little about men. Are you sure you are doing the right thing?"

"It is the *sensible* thing," Geta said obstinately. "Whether it is right or wrong I have to find out for myself. After all, an offer is an offer, however strange it seems!"

Madeline sighed.

"I think you are very brave," she said, "and I shall just be praying that you are not walking into a trap from which it will be impossible for you to escape."

She kissed her sister, and without saying any more left the room.

Geta looked after her, then she walked to the window.

She looked out at the pale Spring sunshine glimmering through the still-leafless trees.

She lifted her face up to it.

"Help me . . . help me," she whispered.

As the sun's rays dazzled her eyes, she was sure that her prayer had been heard.

chapter two

LORD Roydon was sitting at his desk, when a servant approached him.

"What is it?" he asked sharply, annoyed at being interrupted.

"A cable, *Sahib*," the servant replied.

He held it out on a silver salver, and Lord Roydon took it.

There was a faint smile on his face as he realised it was from England.

He opened it and read:

> "SENDING DAUGHTER AS REQUESTED P & O
> BRITANNIA LEAVING TILBURY MARCH 28TH.
>   NAUNTON."

Lord Roydon read it through carefully before he placed it in a drawer.

He had got what he wanted.

He had been, he thought, extremely astute in choosing one of his Cousin Elizabeth's daughters for a wife.

Since he had come to India ostensibly as an Officer in the Army, he had been pursued relentlessly by a great number of women.

Married or unmarried, they were irresistibly attracted to him.

Women had treated him like this ever since he had left Eton.

It was difficult to understand why there was always a slightly contemptuous look in his eyes.

When an *affaire-de-coeur* did not take place, it always ended with the woman in tears.

Then Lord Roydon would go off somewhere without a thought for the broken heart he had left behind him.

He never confided his thoughts or feelings to anyone.

This made him a difficult man to understand.

There was no doubt he was admired, and the Viceroy held him in the highest regard.

Yet few men could boast of knowing him well.

Only Silvius Roydon himself knew the answer.

He had suffered through a woman from the moment his Mother had died when he was only nine.

He had adored her, as she had adored him because he was her only child.

A year after her death his Father had married again.

From the moment she came into his life, his Stepmother had made the small boy's life a misery.

In fact, the only way that Silvius could escape from her cruelty was when he was at School.

He had therefore grown up with a fanatical and obsessive hatred for his Stepmother.

This gradually came to include all other women.

As he came from a great and revered family and was also exceedingly handsome, it was not surprising that as soon as he grew up, there had been women to flatter him.

They had enticed and pursued him relentlessly while he was at Oxford.

When he appeared in the Social World, he became one of the most sought-after young men of his generation.

The wounds inflicted by his Stepmother, however, had gone deep, so that he always suspected the worst of any woman.

While he accepted their favours—and he would not have been human if he had not—what he gave them was entirely physical.

Mentally they were of no importance to him, as they soon realised.

"Do you know, Silvius," one very beautiful woman had said to him, "you have never told me that you love me."

"I never lie," he replied.

She stared at him in astonishment.

"Are you saying that you do not love me?"

"I have never loved any woman," Silvius Roydon replied, "and I have never told any woman that I loved her."

It was a challenge which the Beauty, like a

great number of women after her, could not resist.

Just as she did everything in her power to change his mind, the woman who succeeded her did the same, but failed.

He enjoyed making love to them because he was a very masculine man.

He admired beauty everywhere he found it, and liked the feel of a soft body moving beneath his.

But when he had left the woman in question, he seldom thought of her again.

When the liaison ended, he was quite prepared to start another one.

He never gave a second thought to what had happened before.

Once in India, he had found himself fascinated and absorbed by that mysterious country, just as a great number of Englishmen had been before him.

He realised its great potential.

He also enjoyed, as he had never enjoyed anything before, the exquisite beauty of everything he saw—the children with their huge dark eyes, the women graceful in their colourful *saris*.

The Temples, the Sacred places, and the Palaces of the Maharajahs.

It was like stepping into a Fairy Story.

Yet it had its deep and violent undercurrents into which he was quickly absorbed.

He made a name for himself in a way that was known only to his Commanding Officers and the Viceroy.

They all said there was no-one in the whole

"Great Game" as daring or as brilliant as Roydon.

Perhaps it was the clearness of his perception that enabled him to keep alive when he was within a hair's breadth of losing his life.

Perhaps it was his brilliance in thinking himself into another guise.

It certainly brought him safely through the enemy lines to save hundreds of British soldiers' lives.

Whatever it was, Lord Roydon had become a legend in his own lifetime.

However, what he did could never be spoken of publicly.

That was why the Viceroy, Lord Curzon, had persuaded the Queen to give him a Peerage.

"He deserves a dozen medals for gallantry, Ma'am," Lord Curzon said at a private audience, "but it is impossible ever to put into words, and certainly not to write it down, the value that Roydon had been to us in India."

It was after he had received his Peerage that Lord Curzon had sent for him.

He had travelled to Calcutta, wondering what difficult task was to be given to him this time.

Lord Curzon, autocratic and overwhelming, received him in his Private Study.

"I sent for you, Roydon," he said, "to tell you that I intend to make you Governor of the North-Western Provinces."

Silvius Roydon drew in his breath.

It was something he had always wanted, and it was a territory he knew extremely well.

"No one could govern it better," Lord Curzon went on, "and no-one except yourself is so familiar with the difficulties and problems which beset us on every side."

"Thank you, My Lord, I am deeply honoured," Lord Roydon replied. "I have in fact heard that the Tibetans are encroaching and the Russians are continuing to send spies to see what they can find out."

Lord Curzon smiled.

"I thought you would not let that go unnoticed! But actually the position is very serious and I can think of no-one who could really cope with the problems except yourself."

There was silence for a few seconds before Lord Curzon said slowly:

"There is, however, a condition which you may not like, but which Her Majesty insists upon."

Lord Roydon held his breath.

"It is," Lord Curzon said, "that you should be married."

Lord Roydon stiffened.

Never in the whole of his career had he ever expected to be told that he must marry.

In fact, it was considered an asset in the "Great Game" if those who participated in the dangers and difficulties of it had no such ties, no clinging wife or mistress in whom they might confide.

Those who had taught him had said often enough:

"Women are dangerous! One unwary word on the pillow can cost many lives. Be careful with whom you associate—trust no-one!"

Silvius Roydon had not replied that there was no necessity for him to be given such a warning.

He did not trust women anyway.

He seldom talked to a woman while he was making love to her.

He kept to the "business in hand," so to speak.

He never discussed his own feelings when he was with other men.

They talked of politics, polo, and tiger-shooting.

Other more personal subjects never entered the conversation.

The idea of marriage had never been considered by him.

Despite the innuendos and the pleadings of the women who found him irresistible, he was determined to remain single.

At the moment he was having some difficulty with Lady Irene Waddington.

The daughter of a Duke, she was very lovely.

She had made, when she was only just eighteen, a disastrous marriage.

She had thought herself to be wildly in love.

The man in question had certainly been handsome and, in his uniform, irresistible.

But while Patrick Waddington was a gentleman, he had little else to recommend him.

Almost before their honeymoon was over, Lady Irene realised she had made a mistake.

Her husband was undoubtedly a bore.

When they returned to the Social World they more or less lived their own lives.

It was therefore a great relief when after four years of separate beds, Waddington was killed in a hunting accident.

If he had lived, he would have been a helpless cripple.

However, he died after two weeks of acute pain.

His wife had hardly bothered to visit him.

She was, in fact, having one of her fiery, passionate love-affairs.

It had become the talk of the *Beau Monde*.

The Prince of Wales was among her admirers, as were a great number of rich and charming men.

She then went a little too far where a certain very attractive Peer was concerned.

His wife threatened to divorce him.

The scandal would have caused a sensation, which was extremely undesirable not only from the point of view of the Peer's family, but also because the affair would involve the Crown.

It was the Prince of Wales, therefore, who suggested to Lady Irene that she should visit India.

"Go away, my Dear," he said, "and by the time you come back, the gossips will have found something else to talk about."

"I will do that," Lady Irene agreed, "and as my Father is furious with me, the sooner I am out of his sight, the better!"

"We shall miss your beauty," the Prince said. "At the same time, I feel you will enliven India and find it an extremely interesting part of the Empire."

It was what he had found himself.

Lady Irene knew he was right almost as soon as she set foot in Calcutta.

She, of course, stayed with the Viceroy, and on the first night of her arrival met Silvius Roydon.

From that moment she was aware why fate had sent her to India.

When he was given a Peerage she decided to marry him.

Because he was an ardent lover, she thought there would be no difficulties.

Most of the night before he had received the offer of the Governorship from the Viceroy they had spent in a flame of fire.

Later she said to him in a coaxing tone which most men found irresistible:

"You know, Silvius, I think we were made for each other, and nothing could be more exciting than to be together for ever."

Lord Roydon, who was feeling rather sleepy, could hardly believe what he had heard.

Then, just as when he found himself in a dangerous position on one of his exploits, a little bell seemed to ring in his brain.

He knew he had to tread carefully.

An unwary move could prove to be his death-knell.

That was what it would be now, he thought, if he married Irene.

He could imagine nothing worse than to be tied by the bonds of matrimony, especially to a woman he despised for her promiscuous behaviour.

As a man, he was prepared to enjoy what she was willing to offer.

But a mistress was one thing—a wife was another.

Thinking of his Stepmother, he knew that in no circumstances would he consider giving his name to a woman he did not trust.

To him, she was beneath the surface as revolting as a reptile and as dangerous as a tigress.

Because his brain worked quickly, he yawned before he said:

"I must go back to my own room. I have a meeting at seven o'clock tomorrow morning with the Viceroy, and he does not like being kept waiting."

"I said something important, Silvius," Irene said.

Lord Roydon rubbed his eyes.

"Forgive me, Irene," he answered, "but I really am half-asleep and, as you well know, there is always tomorrow."

"I understood you were leaving Calcutta tomorrow for a visit to Delhi!" Irene said a little sharply.

"Am I?" Lord Roydon asked as he got out of bed. "I am really not thinking straight at the moment, but I expect I shall be given my orders by a tiresome *Aide-de-Camp* at some hellishly early hour."

He slipped on his robe, put on his soft-soled shoes, and would have walked towards the door.

Irene held out her arms.

"Kiss me good-night, Dearest," she said. "I love you, and I shall find it hard to live without your kisses until you come to me again."

Lord Roydon remembered that this was an old trick.

If a woman could encircle his neck with her arms, she could pull him down to her.

It was then impossible to escape.

He therefore simply took Irene's hands in his, kissing first one, then the other.

Before she could say any more, he had left the room, closing the door quietly behind him.

She flung herself back on the pillows, exasperated because he had eluded her.

She felt sure he had heard what she said even though he had pretended not to have done so.

"I *will* marry him!" she vowed. "There is no way he can escape me!"

* * *

Back in his own quarters, Lord Roydon realised, after his interview with the Viceroy, that he had been walking on a tight-rope.

He decided that his affair with Irene was finished.

He had anticipated that Lord Curzon had sent for him because he wished to send him on some dangerous mission to another part of the country.

What had never entered his head was that the Viceroy would tell him to get married.

His astute brain weighed up the position exactly.

He had been offered what he had always wanted—the position as Governor of the North-Western Provinces.

On the other hand, there was the horror of having to be married.

His wife would expect him to be faithful; she would bear his name and eventually his children.

He walked across the room and back again.

He felt that the heat was unbearable simply because he was agitated.

Who could he marry?

That was the decision to be made.

Certainly not Irene.

He was certain she would be cuckolding him with his *Aides-de-Camp*, his friends, his enemies, and any other man who took her fancy.

She would also, he thought, bore him unbearably when they were not actually making love.

Then he realised that of all the women who had passed through his hands since he had come to India, there was not one whom he would consider making his wife.

He thought of the "Husband-Hunters."

He knew that he could not tolerate any of them, however well-born they might be.

They were the women, who, having failed to receive a proposal after several Seasons in London, came out to India.

They had every hope of finding a husband there.

Englishwomen were scarce in India, and there was a profusion of dashing young Subalterns and smart *Aides-de-Camp*.

There were, too, quite a number of visitors who came for the sport and who were usually eligible bachelors.

The "Husband-Hunters," or the "Fishing-Fleet," whichever name you preferred, paraded themselves in front of them.

"Like horses in a Spring sale," someone remarked cynically.

Lord Roydon thought it most distasteful.

He also considered the majority of the young girls plain and stupid.

"Otherwise," he argued, "they would not be in India, but walking up the aisle of St. George's in Hanover Square."

Even as he spoke the words aloud, he remembered his visit to his Cousin, Elizabeth Naunton.

He had always had a great admiration for Sir Reginald.

He had enjoyed the first books he had written enormously.

He had found him one of the most intelligent men to talk to that he had ever met.

Granted they had many tastes in common.

But Sir Reginald had an amusing wit as well as a brain stocked as full as the *Encyclopaedia Britannica*.

Elizabeth Naunton, Lord Roydon thought, had a charm and a sweetness that most women lacked.

She was very feminine yet could hold her own in a conversation.

At the same time, she was a good listener, and she obviously adored her husband.

He could not imagine her being unfaithful to Sir Reginald any more than he could imagine her flying to the moon.

On his last leave in England he had called at Wick House because he was staying with the Member of Parliament for Worcestershire.

The house was not far from the village of Little Wick.

He was impressed by his Cousin, whom he

thought had grown more beautiful since he had last seen her.

He was charmed also by her two daughters.

Dark-haired and with sparkling eyes, they were both outstandingly lovely.

They also had the good manners of their Mother.

They had listened wide-eyed to what he had to say.

He had known that Sir Reginald had educated them in a way very different from the majority of girls in the country.

They were able to talk on the subjects that he found so interesting in their Father.

At the same time, they did not "push themselves forward," or try to attract his attention as a man.

Of course they were young.

He reckoned now that the elder of the two would by now be twenty-one or two.

It was surprising she was not already married.

Her sister, he thought, was doubtless a year or so younger.

Either of them, he decided, would make him exactly the sort of wife he wanted.

He could mould them as their Father had done into behaving the way he wanted.

They would not intrude on him as someone like Irene would do.

Having made up his mind, Lord Roydon acted immediately.

It was something he could not put in a cable.

So he wrote to his Cousin Elizabeth, knowing his letter would reach her in seventeen days.

The opening of the Suez Canal had greatly shortened the long voyages from England to every part of her Empire.

It was now a question of days rather than months.

Lord Roydon thought with satisfaction that he should get an answer by the first week in March.

Having made the decision, he wiped the problem from his mind and concentrated on how he could rid himself of Irene.

Finally, when he had breakfasted, he asked if he could have a word with the Viceroy.

His request was received with some hesitation by those who arranged His Excellency's programme.

But finally Lord Roydon was shown into the Viceroy's Private Sanctum.

"Good-morning, My Lord," Lord Curzon said. "What can I do for you? As I am sure you have been told, I have very little time."

"I just came to tell you, My Lord," Lord Roydon answered, "that I have chosen the young woman I wish to marry and have cabled her to come to India immediately!"

Lord Curzon stared at him, then he threw back his head and laughed.

"You never fail to amaze me, Roydon!" he exclaimed. "Without intruding into your private affairs, I must ask you what you intend to do about that female panther who has already told me she intends to be your wife."

"I was thinking, My Lord," Lord Roydon replied, "that you might have some urgent work for me to attend to which will take me away for the next few weeks to a place which the lady in question would find extremely unpleasant."

Lord Curzon laughed again.

Then, lowering his voice, he said:

"Well, as it happens, I have only learnt this morning that a very urgent problem has arisen . . ."

When he had finished speaking, Lord Roydon was smiling.

"I will see to it at once, My Lord," he said, "and thank you!"

"On your return—and make certain you do return," the Viceroy said, "you can announce your engagement or your marriage, whichever you like, and your appointment to the North-Western Provinces."

Lord Roydon thanked him again.

To the relief of the *Aide-de-Camp* who was waiting outside, he left the Viceroy's Study.

He went upstairs to his bedroom to tell his servant to pack.

At the same time, his brain was racing feverishly over the problem he had just been given.

He was trusting his perception—or, he sometimes termed it, his "Third Eye"—to tell him the first move he should make.

What was important was that no-one should have the slightest idea that he was involved.

* * *

When Irene realised that Lord Roydon had left without saying farewell to her, she was furious.

42

If he had gone to Delhi, she could have joined him there, or in any other well-known place in India.

But apparently he had simply vanished, and when she reproached the Viceroy he merely said:

"Roydon is a very busy man, and he is required in the North in a place which you, my dear, would find exceedingly unpleasant."

Lady Irene would have expostulated, but he went on:

"I have, however, invited a charming guest to meet you tonight, whom I know you will find very attractive. He has told me how much he admired you, and, of course, as you well know, your beauty enriches my dinner-table."

There was nothing Lady Irene could say.

The guest who sat next to her was a substitute, if a somewhat feeble one, for Silvius.

"He will have to come back," she told herself. "Then I will be waiting for him."

* * *

Lord Roydon was not thinking of Lady Irene as the train in which he was travelling sped through the night.

He had boarded it wearing his uniform and looking exceedingly smart.

As it was his right, he accepted a Reserved Carriage, which he had to himself.

The rest of the train was packed to suffocation.

Early the following morning they reached the Junction beyond which the train went no farther.

Only a servant with His Lordship's luggage emerged from his Reserved Carriage.

The train had, of course, stopped at various places on its journey North.

No-one had noticed a *Fakir* with his arms covered with ash moving away from the train.

It was ten weeks later that the secret code known only to the "Top Brass" and guarded night and day by the Military in the ground of Viceregal Lodge received the message:

"Dinner party arranged as requested."

This was interpreted quite simply as

"MISSION ACCOMPLISHED."

chapter three

LINETTE and Madeline were married very quietly in the village Church early in the morning.

There was no-one present except for Geta and the old Parson who had known them since they were born.

He read the Service slowly and sincerely.

The Spring sunshine was coming through the stained glass windows and the birds were singing outside.

Geta thought the quiet Service was very moving, and it was the way she would like to be married herself.

She could see the expression of love in Henry's eyes when he looked at Linette, while the adoration in James's revealed how fortunate both her sisters were.

The men they were marrying loved them with exactly the same love her Mother and Father had shared.

It was what she longed for herself.

'Perhaps,' she thought, 'it is something I shall never know, although, of course, I shall go on hoping.'

She knelt while the Parson blessed her sisters and their husbands.

As she did so, she felt that a Power greater than herself was directing her to where she was going.

Linette and Madeline had begged her over and over again not to go to India.

"I am sure we will be able to find you something interesting to do in London," Linette said. "Once there, you will meet someone by chance, just as I met Henry, and fall in love."

"And suppose I do not?" Geta asked. "Then all my life I would regret not seeing India."

"Seeing India is one thing," Linette replied sharply, "but marrying a man you have never met is something very different."

Geta got up from the chair in which she was sitting to walk to the window.

It was difficult to explain it to her sisters, but somehow she knew instinctively that she was doing the right thing, even though it seemed strange and hazardous to them.

However, she did have qualms at night in bed.

At the last moment she wondered if, after all, she should send a cable to Calcutta saying that Lord Roydon must search elsewhere for a wife.

Then, because it was all happening in such a hurry, there was hardly time to think.

"Henry is buying me a trousseau in Paris,"

Linette said. "So, Dearest, you can have any of my clothes you like."

Madeline said the same, only her reason was a little different.

Her future Mother-in-Law was so delighted that her son was getting married.

She had therefore offered Madeline a trousseau as a wedding-present.

Lady Sheldon was buying her a few things in London which she was sending straight to Cornwall.

It was where they were to spend their honeymoon.

"It is going to be a very long one," Madeline explained, "because, like Linette, I have no wish to look like a black crow, and no-one in Cornwall will know that I am in deep mourning."

She smiled happily as she said:

"James has a house there which was left to him by his Uncle, and there are some excellent horses to ride."

She smiled before she went on:

"We will be away from all the gossips who would be shocked if they realised how quickly we had got married."

This meant that Geta was able to pack quite a number of cases to take with her to India.

She remembered her Father saying that the Indian tailors were brilliant at copying anything they were given.

She thought how exciting it would be to have some of the gowns she now owned copied, using, of course, the lovely materials which could be found only in India.

There were also one or two of her Mother's gowns which could be altered to make them more fashionable.

She therefore said triumphantly:

"I think, although it seems extraordinary, that I have a bigger trousseau than either of you!"

Her two sisters laughed.

"I doubt if it will be grand enough for the 'High and Mighty' gentleman you are marrying," Linette teased. "I am sure he is very fastidious, and perhaps as knowledgeable about women's clothes as he is about pictures and furniture!"

"I suppose that is why Papa liked him," Geta remarked. "He thought that anyone who had good taste in those things would have good taste in everything else."

There was silence.

She knew that both her sisters were thinking it was very bad taste to ask for a wife as if, as they had already said, she were a package to be bought over the counter.

But they both knew there was no point in continuing to upset Geta.

Only when they were alone did Linette and Madeline ask how they could prevent their sister from going to India.

"It is bound to be a 'wild-goose-chase,' " Linette moaned.

"Suppose he makes her miserably unhappy?" Madeline said. "What will she do about it?"

"He cannot be as bad as all that," Linette answered, "and at least she will not shock him, as apparently he has been shocked by the

Englishwomen who go to India."

She was thinking of what Lord Roydon had said in his letter to her Mother.

It had seemed to her a strange thing for a man to say.

But she thought it would be a mistake to talk about it in front of Geta.

After the wedding-ceremony they all went back to the house.

Both Henry Preston and Sir James had carriages waiting to take them to the station.

They had asked Geta to go with them to London.

She refused, because it would have meant her staying with them when all each couple wanted was to be alone.

Instead, after they had left she finished her packing.

Then she drove to the station.

She took a train which would get her into London just at the right time to board the P. & O. Steamer which was leaving Tilbury at nine o'clock.

As had been arranged, Mr. Mayhew, the representative from Thomas Cook's, met her at Paddington Station.

He was a middle-aged man with a kindly face.

Geta had the idea he was a little worried when he saw how young she looked.

"I hope you will be all right, Miss Naunton," he said. "I have arranged for a Clergyman and his wife who are returning to Calcutta after a holiday in England to look after you."

"I am sure that will be splendid," Geta said,

"and it is very kind of you to trouble about me."

"I am afraid they are both a little old for you," Mr. Mayhew said, still in a worried tone, "but I had rather expected you to be older."

"Why should you have expected that?" Geta asked in astonishment.

"The majority of Ladies travelling to India," Mr. Mayhew said, "are either very young and chaperoned by their Mothers or relatives, or else they go out to make a tour of the country and perhaps write a book about it when they come back."

Geta laughed.

"That is something I am sure I shall never be able to do and, as it happens, I am going out to marry Lord Roydon."

She saw no reason why it should be kept a secret.

Then, when she saw the astonishment on Mr. Mayhew's face, she thought she had been indiscreet.

"Then, of course, Miss Naunton, you must allow me to wish you every happiness!" Mr. Mayhew said.

Geta had the feeling that he thought she would need it.

She wondered if she would find Lord Roydon as frightening as her Mother's relatives had told her he was.

She knew, however, that it would be incorrect to ask questions.

They talked of other things until they reached Tilbury.

Everything had been arranged very efficiently.

Geta had been allotted a very attractive cabin on the First Class Deck.

Her luggage was being brought in when Mr. Mayhew told her that the Clergyman and his wife were already aboard.

He took Geta to meet them.

She found Canon Upton and his wife together in the Saloon.

They were, as Mr. Mayhew had said, an elderly couple.

Mr. Mayhew had already informed them why she was going to India, and Mrs. Upton said:

"Of course, my dear, we are delighted to look after you, and we consider it a privilege when you are going out to be married to such an important man."

She glanced at her husband, and the Canon said:

"I heard many things about Mr. Roydon before he became a Peer, and he is very much respected in Calcutta as well as in other parts of India."

Geta thanked them for their good wishes, and Mrs. Upton said:

"I hope, Miss Naunton, that we shall be able to look after you properly on the journey, but I must warn you that neither my husband nor I are very good sailors. We therefore spend a great deal of the time quietly in our cabin."

"You must not worry about me," Geta said reassuringly, "I shall find it very exciting to be at sea."

She also had another idea.

She waited until Mr. Mayhew had left before she went to the Purser's Office.

She was aware she had to go to the Purser for anything she required.

He was a stout, genial-looking man who smiled at everybody as if he were a benevolent Father Christmas.

"Now, what can I do for you, young lady?" he enquired when Geta reached his office.

"I was wondering," she said, "if it would be possible for you to find me somebody on board who would teach me *Urdu*."

The Purser looked surprised.

"That is certainly an unusual request," he said, "but it should not be difficult. There are a great many Indians aboard, but whether they can teach you their language is another matter."

As he was speaking, an Indian came up to the desk and the Purser, turning towards him, said:

"Good evening, Your Highness. Perhaps you would be able to solve a problem for me."

"A problem?" the Indian asked somewhat sharply.

"This young lady wants to learn to speak *Urdu*," the Purser explained, "and I wondered if there might be someone in Your Highness's entourage who could teach her."

"Certainly not!" the Indian said emphatically. "Those who are travelling with me are already fully engaged."

He turned as he spoke and walked away.

The Purser looked ruefully at Geta.

"Obviously I have put my foot in it!" he said. "But there—one never knows with Indians! Some are ready to give you the shirt off their back, others behave like His Highness!"

"Who is he?" Geta enquired.

"He is the Maharajah of Khulipur," the Purser replied.

The name meant nothing to Geta.

As several people came up at that moment to ask the Purser about their luggage, she moved away.

"I will try again tomorrow," she decided.

She felt she had made a mistake in asking for a teacher so quickly.

At the same time, she realised she had only the short time it now took to reach India to learn a little of one of its languages.

Her father had said to her often enough:

"It is useless to go to a strange country unless you can talk the language. That is why, my Dearest, I would like you to be proficient in many languages."

'I am sure now that Papa was right,' Geta thought.

She had not mentioned it to her sisters, but she had made up her mind that when she reached India she wanted to talk to the Indians themselves.

She knew she did not want to listen to a doubtful translation from somebody who was English.

It was dark long before the ship moved out of the dock.

When finally they did so, Geta was prepared to go to bed and sleep.

There had been so much to do those last few days at home.

First she had tidied up the house.

Then she had made lists of all the things which could not be claimed by her Cousin Simon when he took possession.

It was agonising to think of losing the beautiful rooms, with their panelling and marble mantelpieces.

There was also the fine furniture chosen by her Father.

Now it would no longer be theirs.

Geta felt she must go over every room, inch by inch, so that she would never forget any of it.

She felt the same about the garden.

It had been so much a part of her life ever since she was a small child picking daisies on the green lawn.

It was an agony to say good-bye to every tree, every bush, and the little stream which ran through the bottom of the garden.

She was in a different situation from her sisters in that they both were leaving to live in the ancestral homes of their husbands.

These were houses which had been in their families for generations.

'I have nothing,' Geta thought miserably, 'and I shall miss Wick House wherever I am and whatever I am doing.'

They had no idea when their Cousin would be returning from Spain.

Therefore, they had left the keys of the house with the Vicar.

He promised that he would send one of the women in the village in every week to dust and clean it.

They decided that as Cousin Simon had been so casual, they would not pack everything they owned until he returned.

Linette, who would be living the nearer, said she would supervise everything.

"I will make quite certain," she had said, "that anything to which Simon is not entitled is kept for Geta."

"You promise you will not let him have anything that belonged to Mama?" Geta begged. "I would like to think I own something besides the contents of my trunk."

Linette kissed her.

"You shall have everything we can squeeze out of our tiresome Cousin," she replied, "so that when Lord Roydon has a house in England, you can have them there."

"It is a pity that his house was burnt down," Madeline remarked.

Geta was not listening.

She was thinking that if she just had a few things of her Mother's, she would not feel so lonely as she did at the moment.

Once aboard the P. & O. Ship *Britannia*, she told herself that this was an adventure.

It was actually very different from anything she had ever expected to happen to her.

'Papa would have approved,' she thought, 'because I am seeing the world just as he did, and he was always seeking new horizons.'

* * *

When Geta woke up in the morning she found the ship had passed through the English Channel.

The sun was shining through the portholes of her cabin.

Because it was exciting to be aboard, she dressed quickly and went in search of breakfast.

She learned that she was to share a small table with the Canon and Mrs. Upton.

There was, however, no sign of them, and she therefore ate breakfast alone.

Then she went out on deck.

She had never been to sea before.

It was fascinating to feel the ship moving through the green water and watch the gulls flighting overhead.

She walked twice round the deck.

Then she saw that those guests who had appeared were being given cups of warm soup.

Geta wanted to enjoy everything while she could.

She accepted the soup, which she drank before walking this time round the Upper Deck.

She found when she came down again that there were a number of Indian passengers.

Once again she wondered how she could learn to speak *Urdu*.

She decided she must approach the Purser for the second time.

By now it was getting on for mid-day, and as she walked along the First Class Deck, she saw the Maharajah who had spoken so sharply yesterday.

He was sitting in a deckchair beside an elderly woman.

Geta guessed this must be his Mother, as she

looked too old to be his wife.

She thought how graceful the woman looked in her *sari*.

She had a bright-coloured silk shawl draped over her shoulders.

As she watched, a younger woman, who was beautiful and who was also wearing a *sari*, came on deck.

A steward hurried to get her a deckchair, and she seated herself beside the Maharajah.

Without appearing to do so, Geta watched them.

A few minutes later a little boy came running up to them.

He was a very good-looking child of about five or six years old.

He had huge dark eyes in his small face.

Behind him came his *Ayah*, an elderly woman with grey hair.

She remained respectfully in the background while the small boy talked to his parents.

'The Maharajah may be disagreeable,' Geta thought, 'but they are certainly a very picturesque family.'

The small boy, obviously bored by doing nothing, ran to the ship's railing.

He was waving his arms at the gulls as they swooped down near the deck.

No-one was paying any attention to him.

As if he wanted to see the birds better, he climbed up onto the first rung of the railing, then onto the second.

Now his head and shoulders were well above the top of the railing.

He was holding out his arms to the gulls, who swooped down towards him as if they thought he was going to feed them.

Then, as Geta watched, she realised that the ship had begun to roll a little more violently than it had done before.

The small boy, holding up his arms to the birds, might easily topple over into the sea.

Even as she thought it, he leant forward as if to try to catch a passing gull, and she realised he was in danger.

Without thinking, acting on an impulse, she ran towards him.

She reached him just as the ship rolled again, and but for her, the child would have fallen into the sea.

She seized both his hands in hers.

He struggled for one agonising moment as he hung suspended over the side with only the water beneath him.

Geta clung to him desperately, wondering if she was strong enough to haul him back to safety.

Then arms reached out and took the boy from her.

A Steward lifted him back on deck.

The small boy screamed and ran to his Father.

The Maharajah had sprung from his chair when too late he realised what was happening.

"Yer should never 'ave let 'im climb up like that, Sir, as it's dangerous!" the Steward said unnecessarily.

Geta drew in her breath.

It had all happened so quickly.

She could hardly believe that she had managed to save the child.

The Maharajah, holding him in his arms, said:

"How can I ever thank you? You saved my son, and it was very clever and brave of you!"

"I . . . I realised just in time . . . that he was in . . . d-danger," Geta tried to say.

It was difficult to speak, because the Maharanee, having made a deep obeisance to her, was now kissing her hand.

"Thank you . . . thank you!" she said. "How can we ever thank you for what you have done?"

It was difficult to protest that there was no need to thank her when they were all so upset.

Finally Geta found herself sitting beside them while the Maharajah said:

"You are the young lady, I think, who wants to learn to speak *Urdu*. I will teach you myself, as will my wife and my Mother."

The child's Grandmother was still crying into her handkerchief, and all she could say was:

"We might have lost Rajiv . . . we might have lost him!"

"He is safe," the Maharjah said, "and because he is so strong and big for his age, we must find him a younger *Ayah*."

The Maharanee nodded.

"That is sensible," she agreed.

Rajiv was sent away with his *Ayah* because it was his luncheon-time, and now they were alone.

Then the Maharjah said:

"When we arrive in India I wish to express

my gratitude more amply than I am able to do at the moment, but nothing I can give you could compare with what you have given me!"

Geta put up her hands in protest.

"Please," she begged, "if I had not saved your little son, I am sure somebody else would have. He is such a handsome little boy . . . I am so glad he is safe."

"He is my only son," the Maharajah said, "and more precious to me than anything else I possess. If there is anything you want while you are in my country, you have only to ask me."

"Thank you," Geta said softly, "but all I really want at the moment is to learn *Urdu*."

The Maharjah laughed.

"It is a difficult language, but we will try to make sure you are able to make yourself understood by the time you arrive in Calcutta."

That was all Geta wanted.

She thought that nothing could be more fortunate.

Perhaps it was her Karma that she had been in the right place at the right moment.

* * *

As he drove towards the Port, Lord Roydon, although he did not wish to admit it, was feeling a little anxious.

It was one thing to write to England for a girl he had seen only for a short time some years ago.

It was quite another to make her his wife.

He imagined it was Elizabeth Naunton's older

daughter who had come out to him.

He tried to remember her name.

He had a feeling it was a French name, but was not certain.

On the other hand, he could remember that her sister's name was Madeline.

He had, at the time, thought it pretty.

It was typical of Sir Reginald to have given his daughters unusual names.

He would not have expected anything else.

"I imagine that, having lived quietly in an isolated part of Worcestershire, she will be shy and perhaps overwhelmed when she first arrives," he decided. "I must do my best to make her feel at ease."

He thought, at the same time, there would be a great deal he would have to teach her.

That in itself would be a bore.

There were so many things he had to do.

But one of them was more urgent than anything else—to go to Lucknow.

He had got back to Calcutta two days ago.

The Viceroy had been eager to hear the details of what had happened in the "job" he had undertaken.

That he had been completely successful went without saying.

Lord Curzon, however, was insatiably curious, and the two men had talked far into the night.

They had a great deal in common.

George Curzon had attained his overwhelming desire to be Viceroy when he was only thirty-nine.

His enthusiasm, his obsessive desire for work

and to do everything himself, was echoed by Lord Roydon.

They were both entranced by India and its tremendous potentiality.

They talked for a long time about what Lord Roydon had done after leaving the train disguised as a *Fakir*.

Then they turned to more personal matters.

"I guessed you would not want to find Lady Irene here when you returned," Lord Curzon remarked.

"I was hoping you would be aware of that, My Lord," Lord Roydon replied, "and I was very grateful when I learnt that you had sent her to Bombay."

Lord Curzon's eyes twinkled.

"I must have inadvertently made her believe that was where you had gone," he said, "and I think it would be a mistake for you to be here when she returns."

"A very great mistake," Lord Roydon said, "and I have certain suggestions to make to Your Lordship to which I hope you will agree."

The Viceroy had agreed.

As Lord Roydon drove in an open carriage with a Cavalry escort, he could not help wondering if his bride-to-be would not find his behaviour somewhat precipitate.

"I am sure, if nothing else, she will be amenable," he told himself. "After all, those girls living in the depths of Worcestershire will know very little of the world outside. Although she will undoubtedly be extremely well-read and well-educated, she will have had no personal encounter with the world as it is."

As the carriage came down the Quay, he saw that the gangways were already down.

The Steerage and Third Class passengers were disembarking.

He walked up the gangway leading to the First Class Deck.

He wondered if his bride would be waiting for him, or whether he should first find the Purser.

It was then he saw that directly above him on the deck was a party of Indians.

At a glance he recognised the Maharajah of Khulipur, a man he had met on various occasions.

He remembered finding him, as all the English did, a very difficult man to deal with.

He realised he would have to cope with him once he took up his position as Lieutenant Governor of the North-Western Provinces.

The Maharajah's Palace was not far from Lucknow.

The Maharajah was, in fact, noted as being among those who did not accede easily to the English rules and regulations.

As Lord Roydon had no wish to speak to the Maharajah at this moment, he turned towards the Purser's Office.

To his surprise, the Maharajah intercepted him.

"Good-morning, My Lord," he said. "It gives me the greatest pleasure to be able to congratulate you and to offer you my warmest wishes for your happiness."

Lord Roydon looked at him in astonishment.

He thought that the Maharajah must be congratulating him on his Peerage.

But the warmth in his voice seemed to imply something more.

Before he could speak, the Maharajah went on:

"Miss Naunton is waiting for you with my family, and she will explain to you even better than I can, My Lord, the great service she has done me, and how I will be eternally in her debt."

Lord Roydon was astonished into silence.

He could only follow the Maharajah, who walked towards the small party of people standing a few yards away.

As he did so, he was aware that an English girl was amongst them.

But she was not the one he was expecting to see.

He had, in fact, no idea who she was.

He remembered quite clearly that Sir Reginald's elder daughter had been dark-haired and very lovely.

His second daughter had also been dark and as beautiful as her sister.

But the girl waiting beside the Maharanee was fair-haired.

She was also quite different from anyone he had ever seen before.

She was certainly lovely, but in a very different way from what he had expected, in fact, very different from anyone he had ever seen.

He could not explain it to himself, but there was something about her which seemed slightly unhuman.

Although he could not think why, she reminded him for one fleeting moment of the snow on the Himalayas.

The Maharanee was making him an obeisance which he acknowledged by sweeping off his hat.

Then Rajiv's Mother held out her hand.

"We will find it hard, My Lord, to tell you how grateful we are to your future wife for what she had done for us."

It was then that Lord Roydon found himself looking into a pair of green eyes flecked with gold.

He thought they held a distinct question in them.

Despite the turbulence in his mind, he was trying to behave as if nothing particularly strange was happening.

He therefore took Geta's hand.

Raising it perfunctorily to his lips, he said:

"Welcome to India!"

She smiled at him, he thought, nervously.

Then, as if the Maharajah thought he should take charge, he said:

"We must not detain Your Lordship, but I hope to be able to express my grateful and heartfelt thanks on a more suitable occasion."

"Your Highness is most gracious!" Lord Roydon managed to say.

To his surprise, the ladies were kissing Geta good-bye.

Then she knelt down to hug the small Indian boy who flung his arms around her neck.

Still feeling astonished, Lord Roydon escorted Geta down the gangway.

The Viceroy's carriage was waiting.

They stepped into it.

Then Geta waved to the Maharajah and his family, who were watching them from the top of the gangway.

She also waved to the Canon and his wife, to whom she had already said good-bye, but who had only just come up on deck.

Only as they drove away did Lord Roydon find his voice.

"Who are you?" he asked. "I have never seen you before, but I imagine that you must be a relative of Madeline and her sister."

He could still not remember Linette's name.

Geta gave a little laugh.

"I thought you would be surprised to see me!" she said. "But Linette and Madeline were unavailable when your letter arrived. In fact, they are both married!"

She paused before she said:

"You could not have known that Mama had died before you wrote to her."

"Died?" Lord Roydon exclaimed.

"She died very suddenly, although, in fact, she had been taken ill soon after Christmas."

"I am very sorry," Lord Roydon said.

"I miss her . . . more than I can say," Geta murmured.

There was a hint of tears in her voice, and Lord Roydon said quickly:

"I did not know that my Cousin Elizabeth had a third daughter."

"I am the youngest," Geta said, "and I am the only one . . . available."

There was silence.

The horses turned at the end of the Quay, and the Cavalry escort rode ahead and behind them.

Then Geta said:

"How lovely everything looks! Just as exciting as I thought it would be."

"Will you tell me your name?" Lord Roydon asked.

"I am Geta."

"It is a name I have never heard before."

"I was born during Papa's Latin period, and 'Geta' means 'Divine Power.' "

"Is that what you think you have?"

She had a feeling he was mocking her. Without hesitating, she replied.

"If I say 'yes,' you will laugh at me, but if I say 'no,' it will not be strictly true! That is the sort of catch-question which, I am sure, makes people afraid of you!"

Lord Roydon was astonished.

"Afraid of me?" he asked. "Who told you that people were afraid of me?"

"Mama told my sisters it was what her . . . relatives felt," Geta replied. "Perhaps it was . . . wrong of me to repeat it . . . I am . . . sorry."

"There is no need for you to be," Silvius Roydon replied. "However, I find it somewhat bewildering to be meeting a person I did not know existed. Or who is so friendly with the Maharajah of Khulipur, who has always been a difficult man where the English are concerned."

Geta did not speak, and after a moment he asked:

67

"How did you manage it?"

"I . . . just . . . happened to save his son's l-life," Geta explained.

Lord Roydon raised his eye-brows.

"How did you do that?"

"He had climbed up the railing of the deck, and as the ship rolled, he almost fell into the sea, but I managed to catch him."

"Great Heavens!" Lord Roydon exclaimed. "Then it is not surprising that His Highness is grateful!"

"He was very kind," Geta said, "and he and his family have taught me to speak *Urdu*."

Lord Roydon stared at her.

"Is that something you wanted to learn?" he asked.

"Of course! Papa always said one should try to learn the language of a country one is visiting."

"Did you not find it difficult?"

"As a matter of fact, it was easier than I expected," Geta replied. "But then, I have already learned many languages."

They drove on, Geta watching the crowds with joy and excitement.

It was exactly what she had expected they would look like.

As they drove along streets lined with trees in blossom, she thought it was a picture she would never forget.

"Before we arrive," Lord Roydon was saying, "I think I ought to tell you that it is imperative that I take up my position as Lieutenant Governor of the North-Western Provinces as quickly as possible. So I have arranged with the Viceroy that we should be married tonight."

Geta, who was looking at the crowds, turned her face to look at him.

In a voice of sheer astonishment, she repeated:

"To-tonight?"

"I am sure you will understand," Lord Roydon explained, "that whatever else we plan, my work must come first, and I assure you I am vitally needed as quickly as possible in Lucknow."

There was silence.

Geta was remembering her sisters had warned her that she might not have time for second thoughts!

Then she told herself there was no use making a fuss.

What did it matter whether she had to marry Lord Roydon tomorrow, the next day, or tonight?

Aloud she said in what he thought was a very well-controlled voice:

"I suppose it will be a very . . . quiet . . . ceremony."

"It will take place in the Viceroy's Private Chapel," Lord Roydon answered, "and His Excellency will give you away. There will be no other guests with the exception of Lady Curzon and one or two *Aides-de-Camp*."

He waited for Geta to say something, and at last she said:

"Linette and Madeline were married secretly because they were in mourning, and I suppose the same applies to me."

Knowing what he had been afraid she might say, Lord Roydon heaved a sigh of relief.

"It will be for me a very memorable ceremony," he said, "and tomorrow we will leave for Lucknow."

He thought, as he spoke, that he had made no mistake in his choice of a wife.

Geta was raising no protests or causing him any trouble.

"Everything is working out exactly as I planned!" he told himself as they drove on.

chapter four

"SHE is enchanting!" Lady Curzon said to Lord Roydon, who was seated on her right.

As he looked down the table, Lord Roydon thought it was a fair description.

There were only twenty people to dinner.

They had all stood to attention as the Viceroy and his wife came into the Drawing-Room before dinner.

Only as they moved into position did Lord Roydon remember that he had not warned Geta what to expect.

To his surprise, she behaved with perfect dignity, curtsying very gracefully to the Viceroy and the Vicereine.

Nor did she seem at all embarrassed when she was taken in to dinner on Lord Curzon's arm.

Some of the guests might have thought this was strange.

Lord Roydon knew the Viceroy was giving her, as his bride-to-be, his special attention.

Geta had found in her luggage a white gown which she thought was exactly what she wanted as a Bride.

It had belonged to Linette.

Her Mother had bought it for her when she was eighteen and appearing for the first time at a Ball.

It was, therefore, more expensive than anything they could afford later.

Some slight alterations had been necessary, because Geta was smaller in the waist than her sister.

Otherwise it fitted her perfectly.

It had a very full skirt and a *décolletage* draped in white chiffon.

It gave her an ethereal look which Lord Roydon had noted when he first saw her.

He wondered as he looked at her whether she was feeling shy or nervous at sitting next to the Viceroy.

Lord Curzon could, in fact, be very intimidating when people first met him.

But to Lord Roydon's gratification, Geta was chatting away to him and appeared to be perfectly at her ease.

As his hearing was acute, he realised she was talking about Lord Curzon's house in Derbyshire.

It was the famous Kedleston Hall, on which Government House in Calcutta had been modelled.

It was the Earl of Mornington who in 1798

had decided that the Governor's House was not important-looking enough for his position.

He had always been tremendously impressed by Kedleston Hall.

It struck him that his Architect might copy it in Calcutta as nearly as possible.

It had become a joke in England and in Calcutta that when Lord Curzon arrived as Viceroy he remarked: "The pillars at Kedleston are of alabaster while these at Government House are only of lath and plaster."

Lord Roydon was wondering if he was repeating this remark to Geta, and he heard her say:

"It must be thrilling for you to feel in India that you are as much at home as if you were in England. My Father always thought that Kedleston was the most beautiful house he had ever seen with, of course, the exception of our own!"

"I believe your house is Queen Anne," Lord Curzon remarked.

"It is very lovely, but, of course, nothing as large or magnificent as Kedleston. I often thought Papa dreamt that one day, perhaps in some re-incarnation, he would own it!"

Lord Curzon laughed.

Lord Roydon thought with relief there was no need for him to worry about Geta.

It surprised him, however, that anyone so young and unsophisticated should not be more shy and nervous.

But he told himself he knew very little about young girls; in fact, he had always avoided them when possible.

He confined himself to the more sophisticated Beauties, who found him irresistible.

When dinner was finished, they repaired for a short time to one of the huge Drawing-Rooms.

Then, when the Viceroy and Vicereine left, Lord Roydon and Geta followed them.

"Go to your bedroom," Lord Roydon said to Geta, "and you will find a veil there which Her Excellency has lent you."

Geta had been wondering about that.

She knew it would be incorrect to be married without something on her head.

She gave Lord Roydon a smile and ran up the stairs.

The Vicereine's lady's-maid was waiting for her.

On the bed lay a beautiful Brussels lace veil, which she learnt had been worn by Mary Curzon herself at her own wedding.

The maid draped it over Geta's fair hair, not covering her face.

Instead, she let the veil fall to the ground on either side.

Then she produced not a wreath of orange blossom, as Geta had expected, but a small tiara of flowers fashioned in diamonds.

"How very pretty!" Geta exclaimed.

"Her Excellency told me to tell you, Miss, that this is her wedding-present to you."

Geta felt overcome.

She knew the wreath was very becoming.

She looked at herself in the mirror.

Her sisters would approve that she was being married with all the finery customary for a Bride.

Because their marriages had been so secret, Linette and Madeline had worn their best day-gowns.

With them were small hats which they would wear for travelling to London.

"You look lovely, Miss!" the maid said, breaking in on her thoughts.

"I certainly look like a Bride," Geta replied, "except that I have no bouquet."

Even as she spoke, there was a knock on the door.

When the maid opened it, a servant handed in a small bouquet of star-shaped orchids.

'Now I have everything!' Geta thought.

There was another knock, and this time it was Lord Roydon.

He was wearing the evening-clothes he had worn at dinner.

But now his cut-away coat was emblazoned with decorations, one of them a large diamond star.

"Are you ready?" he asked.

He thought as he spoke that it would be impossible for any man to ask for a more beautiful Bride.

Geta moved towards him.

He took her down a side staircase, where there were no servants on duty.

Nor would they be seen there by the guests who were staying in the house.

The Private Chapel was built out at the back.

It was small but beautifully decorated, and the altar was covered with flowers.

When they reached the door into the Chapel,

the Viceroy was waiting there for them, and Lord Roydon walked ahead.

He stood in front of the altar, waiting for his Bride.

The Viceroy gave Geta his arm.

She was intelligent enough to be aware that this was a tribute not to her, but to Lord Roydon.

The Viceroy gave her away in the conventional fashion.

This was something which she knew would impress her sisters when she wrote and told them about it.

The Chaplain read the Service with the same sincerity as the Vicar had done in the village of Little Wick.

But Geta knew, as she listened, that something was missing.

It was the love she had seen in Henry's and Sir James's eyes.

There had been, too, a radiance on her sisters' faces that transformed them.

When Lord Roydon placed the wedding-ring on her finger she could not help remembering how Linette had said he was called "The Icicle."

It flashed through her mind that perhaps he would never love her.

She wondered if the importance of her position as his wife and the joy of being in India would be sufficient compensation.

"I want love," she told herself.

Then she thought perhaps she was asking too much of Fate.

When the Service was over, they went to the Viceroy's Private Study.

A bottle of champagne was waiting for them.

Lord and Lady Curzon drank a toast to their happiness before they withdrew, leaving them alone.

As the door of the Study closed behind them, Lord Roydon said:

"As I expect you know, we have to leave very early in the morning, so perhaps you should go to bed."

"Yes . . . of course, that would be a good idea," Geta agreed. "It has been a very exciting day."

She walked towards the door as she spoke, and Lord Roydon opened it for her.

There was no-one in the corridor outside.

They went up the side staircase by which they had descended to the Chapel.

An Indian maid was waiting for Geta in her bedroom, and Lord Roydon left her at the door.

When he had done so and Geta was undressing, she suddenly realised that he was in the room next door.

She had never thought about it when she had gone upstairs to dress before dinner.

Now she could hear his voice.

He was obviously speaking to the valet who was attending to him.

The maid helped her into a very pretty nightgown which had originally belonged to her Mother.

She obviously expected her to get into bed, and pulled back the sheets.

However, Geta put on the *négligée* which matched the nightgown and fastened it down the front.

She thought the maid was looking at her strangely, and she said:

"There is no need to wait, and thank you for looking after me. Please call me early in the morning, as I must be careful not to keep His Lordship waiting."

The maid seemed to understand, and left the room.

There was no sound coming from Lord Roydon's bedroom.

Geta walked to the window to pull back the curtains and look out over the garden.

The stars were shining overhead, and there was a moon turning everything to silver.

It was a very beautiful sight, but Geta was not really looking at what she saw.

She was wondering if Lord Roydon would come to her room.

It seemed strange that he might do so.

Yet she thought because they were married it might seem even stranger if he did not.

As she waited, the communicating-door, which was between the mantelpiece and the window, opened, and he came in.

He was wearing a long, dark robe.

It was very much like the one her Father had always worn.

When he saw her standing at the window, he raised his eye-brows and asked:

"Not in bed? I thought you were tired."

With an effort, Geta turned to face him.

"I want to . . . talk to . . . you."

Lord Roydon smiled.

"We have had little chance of conversation,

but I feel it is more important that I should kiss my wife for the first time."

"No!"

Geta spoke impulsively, and it was almost a cry.

She saw the surprise on Lord Roydon's face.

She moved past him to sit down in an armchair in front of the fireplace.

As he stood irresolute where she had left him, she said:

"Please . . . I must . . . talk to you."

He moved then and sat down beside her.

For a moment there was silence. Then Geta said:

"I . . . I have been thinking about our . . . marriage . . . and I am afraid you will . . . find me . . . very ignorant . . . as I do not think Mama expected me to be . . . married when I was . . . so young."

"I am quite prepared . . ." Lord Roydon began.

Geta held up her hand to prevent him from saying any more.

"What I have been . . . thinking," she went on, "although, of course, I may be . . . wrong . . . is that while men may want to . . . kiss and t-touch a woman . . . even when they do not . . . love her . . . a woman would not want a man to do . . . either of those things."

She gave Lord Roydon a quick glance, and when he did not say anything, she added:

"Unless . . . she . . . loved him."

Lord Roydon thought there were many ways in which he could argue this point.

However, it was simpler just to nod his head.

"Wh-what I am . . . suggesting," Geta said after a slight hesitation, "is that we . . . wait a little and see if either of us . . . falls in love with . . . the other."

Lord Roydon had the strange feeling that Geta rather than himself had taken charge of the situation.

Choosing his words carefully, he said:

"I quite understand what you are saying to me, and if it is something about which you feel very deeply, then of course I must agree to your suggestion. At the same time, let me say, as I should have done before now, that I find you very beautiful and very attractive."

That was certainly no exaggeration, he thought.

Her fair hair was hanging over her shoulders, and her large eyes were looking up at him questioningly.

She was, as he had thought when he first saw her, different from any other woman he had ever seen.

There was, in fact, something about her—was it spiritual?—that he had never seen in any woman before.

"I am glad . . . you think . . . that," Geta said, "because I was . . . afraid you would be . . . disappointed that I do not look like . . . Linette or Madeline."

"It was certainly a surprise to find you so fair," Lord Roydon answered, "but I am not complaining. In fact, I am delighted that you are as you are and, as I have already said, I want to kiss you."

Geta shook her head.

"I . . . I want you to do that . . . later, but not now . . . when we have only . . . just met . . . each other."

Lord Roydon stared at her before he asked:

"Is it possible that you have already taken a dislike to me?"

He thought, as he spoke, it was something that was quite impossible.

He was so handsome and had for most women a presence that was irresistible.

His advances had never been refused.

In fact, women usually made it impossible for him not to kiss them, however short their acquaintance.

There was a distinct silence. Then Geta said:

"I . . . I have . . . never been kissed . . . but when I am . . . I want to be . . . in love."

"And you think that might be difficult where I am concerned?" Lord Roydon asked.

Now there was a sarcastic note in his voice.

How was it possible that this child, for she was little more, could not be attracted to him?

Already she had the privilege of bearing his name.

Geta rose to her feet.

"Please," she said, "I know it is a . . . mistake for us to . . . argue about anything that is . . . as difficult to translate into words as . . . love . . . I do want to . . . be in love . . . and if we were only . . . pretending it might . . . spoil something . . . very precious . . . which could . . . if we are fortunate . . . come to us . . . in the future."

There was nothing more Lord Roydon could say.

Slowly he rose to his feet.

He wondered what would happen if he swept Geta into his arms and kissed her, as he very much wanted to do.

He thought her lips would be very sweet, tender, and innocent.

He knew as she stood there, looking so lovely, that any man would find her irresistible.

But he knew that if he did such a thing, she might hate him for taking her unawares.

He was too intelligent not to know that he must treat her very gently.

He had to gain not only her confidence and trust, but eventually, if he was patient, her love—the love which for her was different from that of the women who had desired him with a fiery passion that often seemed insatiable.

Aloud he said:

"I will be frank, Geta, and say that this is not at all what I expected on my wedding-night. But because I want to make you happy and because I need your assistance in the work I have to do in this country, I will agree to what you have suggested."

"Thank you," Geta said with a sigh of relief, "thank you very much, and I promise I will try to do . . . everything you want of me . . . especially where it concerns your work in India."

"That starts tomorrow morning," Lord Roydon said, "so go to bed now. There will be many excitements ahead of you when we reach Lucknow."

He was standing facing her.

He wondered if he should take her hand and kiss it.

Then, as she did not move, he turned to walk towards the communicating-door.

Only as he reached it did Geta say in a small, child-like voice which was different from the way she had been talking previously:

"You . . . you are not . . . angry with . . . me?"

Lord Roydon smiled and shook his head.

"Not in the slightest!" he said. "Only a little disappointed."

He left the room as he spoke, shutting the door behind him.

Geta stood still for several minutes before she closed the curtains and crept into bed.

Only as she lay in the darkness did she ask herself what he meant when he said he was disappointed.

'Perhaps he really did want to kiss me,' she decided.

* * *

When the morning came, Lord and Lady Roydon drove away from Government House in great style.

There was a Cavalry escort both in front and behind them.

Their luggage followed in charge of Lord Roydon's valet.

When they arrived at the station, Geta found they had been lent the Viceroy's private train to carry them to Lucknow.

This was another concession to Lord Roydon's importance.

Geta was delighted at the comfort of the red and white train with its elegant Drawing-Room.

There were stewards to wait upon them as they sat in the comfortable armchairs.

There were two sleeping-carriages.

Geta felt a little embarrassed at taking the larger of the two.

There was so much to see along the way and so many questions for her to ask that the journey passed quickly.

She was amazed by the crowds on the station-platform.

The Indians lived and slept there sometimes for days before they boarded a train.

They often had with them not only a multitude of children, but also their goats and dogs.

The Officials at every station came to greet Lord Roydon.

Geta was impressed by how important he was to them.

By the time they reached Lucknow, Geta felt that she had learnt a great deal about it from Lord Roydon, far more than she could ever have learnt from books.

She knew it was originally the Capital of the Kings of Oudh.

He told her that it was known as a city dedicated to pleasure, besides being renowned as growing the most beautiful roses in India.

Lord Roydon was about to add:

" . . . and the best Nautch Girls."

Then he remembered to whom he was speaking.

It would be a mistake to have to explain to

Geta what a "Nautch Girl" was, and what she was expected to do.

Geta's previous knowledge of Lucknow was confined to the siege that had taken place at the time of the Mutiny.

It had left the Governor's House nothing but a shambles.

Now it had been rebuilt and added to by each subsequent Governor, and was very comfortable.

At the same time, she could not help feeling that the spirit of courage and endurance shown in the siege still lingered in it.

It was that which had kept alive women and children as well as soldiers, many of them severely wounded.

Their unquenchable will was still part of the place.

She felt it vibrating in the atmosphere around her when she walked in the garden.

From the moment they arrived she found it almost impossible to talk to or be alone with her husband.

First of all, there were a great number of inauguration ceremonies in which they were both required to take part.

Then, as was to be expected, everybody of importance in the neighbourhood came to call on the new Governor.

They paid their respects to him personally and were taking a long time about it.

Geta might have felt herself forgotten.

On the fourth day, however, after their arrival, she was told there was a special messenger waiting for her.

He had a parcel which had to be handed to her personally.

Curious, she asked for the man to be brought to her presence.

When he appeared, she knew by his very elaborate uniform that he represented one of the Indian Maharajahs.

In fact, she was not really surprised when she learnt that he had come from the Maharajah of Khulipur.

Bowing deeply, then going down on one knee, he presented her with a large velvet box which he said came with His Highness's good wishes and blessings for her future happiness.

Geta thanked him, and having told one of the servants to look after him before he returned to his Master's Palace, she opened the gift he had brought to her.

When she saw what it contained, Geta could only gasp in astonishment.

Forgetting protocol, she ran down the corridor to Lord Roydon's Study.

He had already been in consultation with a dozen different people every hour of the day.

There was an *Aide-de-Camp* outside the door, and she asked:

"Is His Excellency alone?"

"I think His Excellency's visitors are just leaving," the *Aide-de-Camp* replied.

Geta smiled.

"Then I will wait. I hope they will not be long."

To her delight, the door opened and the visitors came out to be escorted back to their carriages by the *Aide-de-Camp*.

When the last of them had passed her, Geta ran into the room.

Lord Roydon was sitting at his desk, and he looked up in surprise when she appeared.

"I know you are busy," Geta said breathlessly, "but I have something to show to you, and I know you will be as astonished as I am when you see it!"

She put the velvet box down on his desk and opened it.

As she had drawn breath at the first sight of it, she was not surprised when her husband was silent.

Then he said:

"I suppose it comes from the Maharajah of Khulipur!"

"He said he would give me a present," Geta answered, "but surely I cannot accept this?"

It was certainly an amazing gift.

There was a necklace of rubies, diamonds, and pearls set in the exquisite tradition of Indian craftsmanship.

Besides the necklace, there were two bracelets and ear-rings to match it, also a headband of the same stones.

In the centre of this there was one huge ruby.

"It must be worth a King's ransom!" Geta gasped.

Lord Roydon did not speak.

Then after a moment he replied:

"That is a good description, because the Maharajah is proud of being descended from the Kings of Oudh."

"I cannot accept such a valuable present!"

"He will be deeply offended if you refuse," Lord Roydon said, "and it would be a great mistake to 'look a gift-horse in the mouth!' "

Geta gave a little laugh.

Then she said:

"Now at least, if I run away I shall not starve, or have to earn my living by cleaning floors!"

"Are you thinking of running away?" Lord Roydon asked.

"Not now, but I did think of it before I reached India, when I assumed I would have time to consider the position before I was actually married."

"And now there is no escape!" Lord Roydon said. "Are you quite certain you do not want one?"

His eyes were on her profile as she looked down at the tremendous gift she had received.

He was wondering what she would reply.

"I am finding India entrancing," she said at length. "Even before this came I thought it had given me something very special that I must not lose."

Lord Roydon smiled a little wryly.

He understood what she was saying, but he realised that he did not come into the picture.

It was India that was holding Geta captive, not himself.

An *Aide-de-Camp* came into the room.

"Excuse me, Your Excellency," he said, "but your next visitors have just arrived."

Geta picked up the velvet box and closed the lid.

"I would have liked to talk to you about this,"

she said, "but there never seems to be time."

"It will be easier," he replied, "when we go up to Naini Tal."

"Are we going there soon?" Geta asked eagerly.

"It is already unprecedentedly hot for the time of year," Lord Roydon replied, "and as I have so far been deprived of a honeymoon, I intend to go there as soon as it is possible for me to get away."

Geta smiled at him.

There was a great deal she wanted to ask about Naini Tal.

But at that moment she realised that her husband's visitors were advancing down the corridor.

Quickly she left the Study.

Only when she was upstairs in her own room did she tell herself that she really wanted to talk to the man she had married, not about themselves, but because he knew so much more about India than she did.

There were a million questions she wanted to ask him.

'If we go on like this,' she thought, 'I shall find it hard to recognise him when I meet him in the corridor!'

*　　*　　*

Later that afternoon she was told that she had a visitor.

It was not the usual deputation of women who already took up quite a lot of her time.

When she went into the Drawing-Room, it was to find an elderly lady who was introduced to her as Mrs. Allan.

As Geta shook her by the hand, she wondered who the woman could be, also why the *Aides-de-Camp* had not warned her about the visit.

"I expect you have been told," Mrs. Allan said, "that I am the wife of Dr. Allan, the Chief Medical Officer in Lucknow."

"No, I did not realise that," Geta said, "but, of course, I am delighted to meet you."

"I wanted to meet you," Mrs. Allan said, "because my husband has known His Lordship for many years. Before we came to India, we lived in Staffordshire, near the house where your husband was born."

Geta was instantly interested.

She had never met any of Lord Roydon's family, and thought it rather strange.

She ordered tea, then sat down beside Mrs. Allan, saying:

"Do tell me about my husband's home. He has not talked about it, but I know it was burnt down and I have often wondered how such a catastrophe could have taken place."

Mrs. Allen looked at her in a strange manner.

Then she said:

"I suppose nobody has told you of the gossip there was at the time. It was believed the fire was a deliberate action on the part of your husband's Stepmother."

"A deliberate action?" Geta exclaimed. "How extraordinary! Why should she have done that?"

"Perhaps I ought not to talk to you like this," Mrs. Allan said, "but because both my husband and I were devoted to Mrs. Roydon, your husband's Mother, we were naturally appalled and deeply upset by the way his Stepmother made her small Stepson so unhappy."

"Do you mean . . . she was . . . cruel to him?" Geta asked.

It was then that Mrs. Allan told her of how Silvius Roydon had adored his Mother.

When she had died of peritonitis, for which there was no cure, he had been broken-hearted.

"Everyone's heart went out to the small boy," Mrs. Allan said. "He was so handsome and so charming, and there was no-one in the whole County who did not wish to comfort him."

"And what happened?" Geta asked.

"Colonel Roydon, who had been a distinguished and very brave soldier, married again. She was a beautiful woman in her own way, but hard and very unsympathetic. She seemed to take a dislike to her Stepson, I think because she could have no children of her own."

Mrs. Allan wondered if she should tell Lady Roydon of the taunts to which the small boy was subjected, how he was prevented from riding his favourite horse and how his Stepmother had his dog put down simply because of his fondness for it.

Although she did a million things to hurt the boy, his Father was unaware of it, or else he thought it a mistake to interfere.

"She changed young Silvius from a happy boy into a young man who seemed to withdraw into himself," Mrs. Allan went on.

Geta was beginning to understand why Lord Roydon was known as "The Icicle" and "The Rock."

"He was very clever," Mrs. Allan said, "top of the School, and he gained a good degree at Oxford, but those who loved him felt there was something missing. It was only someone like myself who was sure it was because he had never found anybody to take his Mother's place in his life."

She smiled at Geta as she said:

"That is why I was so glad when I heard he had married and that his wife was not one of those sophisticated Social women whom we have out here and who, as I have always told my husband, are as 'hard as nails!' "

She put her hand over Geta's as she said:

"You are just the sort of wife he should have. You remind me of his Mother, and a lovelier lady never walked this earth."

"Thank you," Geta said. "It is very kind of you to tell me this."

She hesitated before she said:

"Do you really think that my husband's Step-mother burnt down the family house?"

"She was furious when the General died and it was not left to her. It was entailed, like all such properties, onto young Silvius."

She paused a moment and then went on:

"After she had packed all her belongings and driven away in a carriage, there was a mysterious fire that started in the attics but which was not discovered until very late at night. By the time help came in the shape of the Fire-Engine and workers from the Estate, the house was nothing but a shell."

"It is the most horrible story I have ever heard," Geta said.

She knew now why her husband had chosen to include in his title the name of her Father's house rather than what had once been his own Estate.

As if Geta had spoken aloud, Mrs. Allan said:

"With no house in which to live, there was no point in Silvius Roydon keeping on the land. I often wonder when he retires where he will live in England."

"Well, he is not ready to retire yet," Geta said.

"I know it has delighted him to have been made Governor of the North-Western Provinces, and we are very proud to have him," Mrs. Allan said. "My husband has told me how warmly he is spoken of by the Viceroy, and I only hope he will take no risks."

She smiled before continuing:

"There is always danger lurking somewhere in India, especially anywhere near the North-West Frontier."

Geta was to learn this was true later that evening.

She wanted to talk to her husband about the gift from the Maharajah.

She also wanted to show the letter of thanks which she had written in his own language.

Geta went along the corridor to the Study.

There was no *Aide-de-Camp* outside the door, and she had a little feeling of delight that she would find her husband alone.

She turned the handle of the door, then, as she did so, she heard a voice.

"We have alerted everyone to the danger, My Lord," the man was saying. "Of course we have no idea of where or when they may approach us."

Geta was still and did not attempt to move away.

"Do we ever know?" she heard her husband reply in a tired voice.

"You must be careful, My Lord, and for God's sake, take no chances!" his visitor went on. "You know that you yourself can take no part in this."

"That is going to be difficult," Lord Roydon answered.

Now there was a hint of laughter in his voice.

"It is no joking matter, My Lord," his visitor insisted. "They will stop at nothing to get you, and you must, at all times, be protected."

"I am going up to Naini Tal as soon as possible," Lord Roydon answered.

"It may be better there," the visitor conceded. "At the same time, we cannot afford to lose you! Take no chances, and double your guard at night. I will send with you our most experienced men, who have worked with you before."

"Thank you," Lord Roydon said.

"And once again, remember, you are now the Governor. You must let somebody else do the dirty work."

Lord Roydon laughed.

"I have got the message!"

There was the sound of a chair being pushed back.

Geta realised that she had been eaves-dropping.

Quickly she moved away from the door and ran down the corridor.

Only when she reached her own Sitting-Room did the whole import of what she had heard sweep over her.

Silvius was in danger—deadly danger!

She knew that it was connected with the work he had done in India.

It was also the way he was spoken of mysteriously and almost with bated breath.

'I must help him,' she thought.

Instinctively her thoughts went to the Power which she had felt before, the Force which she knew had brought her to India.

It was something that could not fail her now.

What was vitally important was that she must not fail the man to whom she was married.

chapter five

GETA came back from the Bazaar delighted with her purchases.

She had gone with an *Aide-de-Camp* in a Government carriage.

Needless to say, she had created a great deal of interest.

The Shop-keepers were only too willing to sell her anything she required.

She found it difficult not to be extravagant.

She had already planned to surprise her husband that evening with a new gown.

It was so long since she had one that it was a tremendous thrill to realise that, for the first time in years, she was having something new, and made in the most exquisite material she could imagine.

She had bought the material just a week ago.

It seemed incredible that the tailor, or *darzi*, could have copied her wedding-gown so exactly and in such a short time.

The material she had found in the Bazaar was the very pale green of her eyes.

She thought it would look cool as the days grew hotter.

Also, because it was embroidered exquisitely, it would shimmer when she walked.

"I will wear it tonight as a surprise," she told herself as she drove back to Government House.

She had also bought some material for the *darzi* to make another gown.

This time he was to copy one of Linette's which Geta had always thought particularly becoming.

There was no sign of Sylvius.

She knew he was out on an inspection of some sort and there was no knowing when he would return.

She only hoped he was properly guarded.

She was still frightened by the conversation she had overheard about his being in danger.

Every time he was late in coming home, she felt her heart beat in a frightened manner in case something had happened.

She would have liked to discuss it with him.

But then she would have had to reveal that she had eaves-dropped at his door.

She was sure it would annoy him.

It might also seem as if she were intruding upon his private affairs.

When she thought it over, she knew that he had been part of what was known as the "Great Game."

Her Father had mentioned it to her once or twice when they were talking about India.

She had not been particularly curious about it then.

Now she had begun to understand more from little things that were said.

It was, in fact, a most brilliant Secret Service organisation on the part of the British to protect the North-West Frontier.

Everybody was aware that the Russians were causing trouble in Afghanistan and also in Tibet.

Piecing together little bits of information, Geta learnt that men like Silvius were adventurous enough to disguise themselves in many different ways.

They could then find out what the Russians were planning.

In many cases they forestalled the destruction of British Troops.

It was just the sort of thing, she now knew, that Silvius would do.

Yet, she had not at first connected him with anything so dangerous or unusual.

Almost like the Viceroy, he seemed too impressive, too autocratic, to take part in what was called a "Game."

Yet every move in it was a risk to his own life.

She knew now that with one unwary word, one slip, not only would men die, but the vital information which had been gained would also be lost.

She found herself looking down the table at Silvius at meal-times.

She wondered if he, who made other people afraid, was ever afraid himself.

The Russians in their determination to occupy

India were completely ruthless towards anyone they considered their enemy.

Quite suddenly Geta was desperately afraid for Silvius.

She had never been afraid for anyone before in her quiet, uneventful life.

She remembered that his visitor had said he was to play no part in what was happening.

But she had the feeling that he would not be able to avoid it when the occasion arose.

When they went to bed she looked to see that there were plenty of sentries on duty.

She thought that the *Aides-de-Camp* were of more assistance than usual.

They dashed to see if the windows were closed and the doors locked as soon as she and Silvius retired for the night.

'If only I could talk to him about it,' she thought.

Once again she was afraid that he might consider it an intrusion.

The *darzi* was waiting on the verandah.

When Geta saw the gown he had finished, she gave a cry of delight.

It was certainly very beautiful.

As he held it up, the sunshine glittered on the silver thread running through the material.

She was sure it would become her more than any gown she had ever worn before.

"Thank you! Thank you!" she exclaimed in *Urdu*. "You have been very clever."

The *darzi* smiled at the compliment.

When she paid him, she gave him the new material she had bought in the Bazaar together with the gown she wanted him to copy.

He was delighted that he had been given another commission.

He settled down at once, cross-legged, to take a pattern.

In her own room Geta went to her desk to look at the programme for the day.

Every morning an *Aide-de-Camp* handed her a programme.

Everything in which she was concerned, that was to take place during the day, was written down.

Already there had been two deputations during the morning.

She had taken her husband's place because he was otherwise engaged.

At luncheon they had received a large number of dignitaries from the city.

Now she saw with a sinking of her heart there was also a dinner-party that night.

There were a number of important guests who had not been invited before.

"Why can we never have an evening alone?" she asked angrily.

Then she knew it was impossible while Lord Roydon was still, as it were, "playing himself in" in his new position.

But, at least, Geta thought, she would have an audience for her new gown.

Because she was tired after the heat and the crowds in the Bazaar, she undressed and lay down on the bed.

There was a pile of books on one side of it which she was enjoying.

They all were concerned with India and answered many of the questions she was unable to ask her husband.

But for the moment she was content just to lie and think.

The sun-blinds were drawn over the windows.

It was not quite as hot as it had been earlier in the afternoon.

At the same time, she was very glad of the air coming from the *punkahs*.

These were worked from outside the room by a native servant.

She must have fallen asleep, for she awoke with a start.

Lord Roydon's valet was standing by her bed.

"It getting late, Lady *Sahib*," he said, "and Lord *Sahib* ask me tell you not be late, as very important people for dinner tonight."

"Thank you for waking me, Kumar," Geta said as she smiled.

She liked the man who had been with Lord Roydon for many years.

She guessed, too, that he had been involved in many of his Master's strange missions.

She longed to talk to him about it, but knew it was something she must not do.

There was a cool bath waiting for her in the closet which opened out of her bedroom.

After her bath she started to dress, knowing, as every other woman knows, the joy of wearing a new gown for the first time.

Kumar had already trained one of the men-servants to wait on her as efficiently as he waited on her husband.

Lord Roydon had explained to Geta that it was a mistake to have women in the house.

It was something that had never happened in the past except for the *Ayahs* for the children.

He did not say so, but Geta thought one reason was that they were afraid women would talk.

There were too many dangerous secrets in Government House for them to be bandied about in the Bazaar.

She found that Kumar's trainee, whose name was Janar, was efficient.

He washed and pressed her clothes far better, she thought, than any English lady's-maid would have done.

She called him to do up her gown, and he buttoned it deftly at the back.

As she looked at herself in the mirror, he exclaimed:

"Lady *Mem-Sahib* very smart!"

"I hope everyone thinks so," Geta replied.

She went downstairs hoping she would have a chance of finding Silvius alone.

But already four of the people who were staying in Government House were in the Drawing-Room with him.

There was a General with his wife, and an *Aide-de-Camp*.

The fourth was a distinguished soldier on his way to take up a command on the North-West Frontier.

As Geta moved towards them, she was aware of the admiration in their eyes.

Almost involuntarily she looked at Silvius.

As usual, he had an enigmatic look which she found difficult to read.

The more she saw him, the more difficult it was to know what he was thinking and feeling.

She kept remembering what Mrs. Allan had told her.

She found herself lying awake at night, thinking how he had hated his Stepmother, who had been so cruel to him.

She was sure it had made him encompass himself with a reserve that was like armour.

"What does he feel about me?" she asked herself.

She had no clue to the answer to that question.

More people arrived.

Most of them had permanent posts in Lucknow, or else were on their way farther North or West.

The latter were staying in the house.

Because people came and went with such rapidity, Geta had given up knowing how long her guests were staying or even when they were arriving.

She left it to a very efficient Adjutant.

He had worked for the last Governor and made it quite clear he did not require her help.

Several more guests arrived.

Geta was just thinking that the party was complete, when a servant announced:

"Lady Irene Waddington, Lord *Sahib*!"

Lord Roydon turned round in astonishment.

Geta saw he was surprised, and wondered who the woman was who had arrived so late.

She was, without exception, the most fantastic person she had ever seen.

Very beautiful with flaming red hair, she, too, was wearing a green gown.

Hers was the deep green of an emerald.

Stones to match it glittered around her long neck and in her ear-lobes.

The lower part of her skirt was decorated with feathers of the same colour.

She moved towards Lord Roydon, holding out both her hands.

In a voice that seemed to lilt through the room she exclaimed:

"Silvius! Say you are pleased to see me, and I have only managed by a hairs breadth to arrive on time!"

She put her hands on his shoulders and looked up at him, her red lips very near to his.

"Irene!" Lord Roydon exclaimed. "I cannot imagine where you have sprung from, or why you are here!"

Lady Irene gave a cry which again seemed to echo through the room.

"You did not get my letter? Oh, Silvius, you were not expecting me? How could I have guessed—how could I have imagined—that this would have happened? Except that the Indian posts are abominable!"

Lord Roydon knew her too well not to be aware that she was lying.

He realised she must have arrived just a short time before dinner.

She would have informed the Adjutant that she was staying in the house.

Now there was little he could do, in fact nothing, to prevent her from being his guest.

"It is certainly unexpected to find you here," he said, "in Lucknow. What brings you so far North?"

He knew the answer even though he asked the question.

Lady Irene looked at him from under her eyelashes.

"You know the answer, Silvius," she said in a low voice. "And now, as I am here, even if an unwanted guest, you must introduce me to your charming friends."

"Let me first," Lord Roydon said, "present you to my wife."

He knew, as he spoke, that Lady Irene was well aware that he was married.

She had deliberately come to Lucknow in order to make trouble.

There was, however, nothing he could do except move towards Geta and say:

"Let me, my Dear, introduce Lady Irene Waddington, whose letter informing us of her arrival has unfortunately been lost in the post."

Geta held out her hand, but Lady Irene chose to ignore it.

She only stood looking at Geta with an expression in her eyes that was not difficult to interpret.

"I am naturally very curious to know, Lady Roydon," she said, "what bait you used to capture the most elusive and determined bachelor in the whole of India."

It was rude and offensive.

At the same time, spoken by Lady Irene it somehow sounded witty and amusing.

One or two of the guests laughed.

Then, before Geta could reply, Lord Roydon briskly moved Lady Irene away.

He introduced the General's wife, the General, and a number of other guests.

Geta could hardly believe what she had heard.

Although she had never met anyone like Lady Irene before, she knew perceptively that she was an enemy, and a dangerous one!

There was no mistaking from the way she had looked at Silvius when she arrived what she felt about him.

It suddenly struck Geta that this was the sort of woman he had referred to in his letter to her Mother.

He had said that the English women in India shocked him.

At the same time, Lady Irene was beautiful—breathtakingly beautiful.

It was obvious that the younger men in the party were gazing at her as if bewitched.

Dinner was announced.

The Adjutant, having changed the seating after Lady Irene's arrival, had quite correctly put her on the Governor's right.

And it was Lord Roydon who escorted her into dinner.

From the other end of the table Geta could see exactly how Lady Irene was behaving.

With an expertise and a brilliance Geta could not help admiring, she was flirting with Silvius.

She did so with every word she said, every

movement of her white shoulders, and every flicker of her eye-lashes.

'She is beautiful and she is infatuated with him,' Geta thought. 'I wonder why he did not marry her?'

It occurred to her that this was perhaps the reason he had written to her Mother asking for a wife.

She was sure that Lady Irene would have glittered and shone as the wife of the Governor of the North-Western Provinces.

She would also, Geta thought, perform the task very much better than she could herself.

She tried, because she knew it was what her Mother would have expected, to interest herself in the gentlemen on either side of her.

The General, however, who was on her right, took a very long time to tell a story.

The Judge, who was on her left, kept looking down the table at Lady Irene.

It made a break in what he was saying while he did so.

Geta was also aware that the ladies at the table were all watching Lady Irene.

They had, as she would have described it to her sisters, "their eyes on sticks."

'They will certainly have something to talk about tomorrow,' she thought.

The ladies moved into the Drawing-Room.

Lady Irene first powdered her nose from a small gold powder-box.

Then she deliberately seated herself next to Geta.

"As you can imagine, Lady Roydon," she said,

"I am longing to hear all about you, and why I have not met you before. Since I have been in India I have, as it happens, seen a great deal of your charming, handsome husband."

"This is my first visit," Geta said quietly.

"I find it hard to understand why he did not tell me you were arriving," Lady Irene said. "We were such very *close* friends. I thought I knew all the women in whom he was interested or— should I say?—were interested in him!"

Geta could feel Lady Irene's enmity and malice pouring out of her.

"And where have you come from?" Lady Irene went on. "Was it from England, or did you come out with the Fishing Fleet?"

Geta rose to her feet.

"I am sure my husband will want to tell you all these things himself," she said quietly. "As it happens, my Mother was a Cousin of his, so of course there is nothing very strange about our being acquainted with each other."

She walked away before Lady Irene could reply.

As she did so, she felt the anger in Lady Irene's eyes boring into her back.

It was a relief when the gentlemen joined the ladies.

They appeared somewhat earlier than usual.

For Lord Roydon was well aware that Lady Irene, if given the chance, would tear his wife into pieces.

How could he have imagined, he asked himself, that once she knew he was married, Lady Irene would follow him to Lucknow?

And, what was more, would force herself on his household?

Too late, he recalled the old adage about "a woman scorned."

He thought now it would have been more prudent if he had written to Irene, telling her he was to be married.

She must have been furious at hearing it second-hand.

He had deliberately not made any public announcement in the newspapers.

He wanted to avoid it being known that Geta had been only recently bereaved.

A long period of mourning had been set by Queen Victoria.

It was considered extremely heartless if a family did not wear black for at least a year following the death of a relative.

Geta had already told him that because they had so little money, she and her sisters did not put a notice in the *Morning Post* or *The Times* about her Mother's death.

"Mama had few relatives left," she said, "and both Linette and Madeline wished to be married quickly."

"I agree that was very sensible of you," Lord Roydon replied.

At the same time, he knew that really he had been under an obligation to inform Lady Irene.

He knew she would be annoyed at his having escaped her clutches.

Yet he had never envisaged for one moment that she would follow him to Lucknow.

Because she was determined to do so, Lady

Irene managed to manoeuvre him into a corner of the Drawing-Room.

It was impossible for him to escape.

"I miss you, Silvius," she said in soft, seductive tones which many men found enchanting.

When Lord Roydon did not answer, she added:

"There is a lot we have to say to each other."

The way she spoke and the way she looked told him, incredible though it seemed, what she wanted.

"I am a married man, Irene," he said quietly.

"To that little milk-sop? Do you really think she can hold you, or delight you as I have been able to do?"

He did not reply, and after a moment she said:

"The fire you ignited so skilfully, Silvius, is still burning. I shall be waiting for you."

She turned away before he could tell her that he had no intention of going, as she expected, to her bedroom.

Because in India when dinner was finished the guests who were not resident left immediately, Lord Roydon was busy saying good-bye.

When only the house-guests remained, he signalled his *Aide-de-Camp.*

They went to the door so that he and Geta could retire first.

The ladies curtsied, the gentlemen bowed, and they went from the Drawing-Room and up the stairs.

Only as they reached the landing did Lord Roydon say:

"I must congratulate you on your gown tonight, Geta. I realise it is a new one."

"I did so hope you realised that," Geta answered. "It was made by the *darzi*, and he had copied my wedding-gown very skilfully."

"You look as if you have come from the trees that surround your house at home," Lord Roydon said unexpectedly.

"Do you really think that?" Geta asked. "Those trees mean so much to me. When I said good-bye to them, it was impossible for me . . . not to . . . cry."

They reached the door of her room, and Lord Roydon said:

"When you go to sleep tonight, think of those trees and forget anything unpleasant which is not worth remembering."

He had walked to his door before she could reply.

When she went into her bedroom she thought it a strange thing to say.

Then she realised he had been aware of how unpleasant Lady Irene was being to her.

'I suppose she is jealous,' Geta thought as she undressed.

Then she told herself that if Lady Irene were in her position as Silvius's wife, he would not be sleeping alone in the next room.

For the first time since they had been married, Geta wondered if she had made a mistake.

Perhaps she should not have prevented him from kissing her.

She should not have insisted that they should be in love before she became his wife in the true sense of the word.

She had seen the expression in Lady Irene's

dark eyes as she looked up at Silvius.

She thought that with every movement of her lips there was an invitation.

Even when they were sitting at dinner she was touching his arm or his hand and moving unnecessarily closer to him.

"I hate her! She is like some evil reptile!" Geta exclaimed suddenly.

Yet it was impossible not to admire her beauty and the flamboyance.

She had held the whole room spellbound when she entered it.

Geta thought she herself must have looked very insignificant in her green gown that was like the trees in the garden at home.

How could something made by the *darzi* on the verandah compete with the emeralds round Lady Irene's white neck?

Feathers fluttered as she moved, and there was the glint of fire in her red hair from the light of the candles.

"I hate her! I hate her!" Geta cried again.

Then, to her surprise, she heard the communicating-door between her room and that of Silvius open.

*   *   *

Lord Roydon, having been helped to undress by Kumar, blew out the candles.

Because he was tired, he tried to go to sleep.

But he could not stop himself from thinking about Irene and how she had forced herself upon him as a guest.

She had made it quite clear that she had every intention of resuming their love-affair whether or not he had a wife.

Her type of woman, he thought, had no pride when she wanted a man.

Irene was determined to hold him with the desires of the flesh, in which she was an expert.

Yet he had known as soon as she arrived that she no longer held any attraction for him.

All he felt was the contempt he had felt in the past for all women.

The wounds inflicted upon him by his Stepmother had gone deep.

Now he was worrying as he had never worried before that Irene might hurt Geta.

She would undoubtedly shock and disgust her.

He had no wish for Geta even to guess to what depths of depravity he had sunk with Irene.

For the first time in his life, Lord Roydon was concerned over a woman's feelings.

Geta was so young, so unspoilt, and so completely innocent.

He could not bear the idea of her being defiled by a woman like Irene.

'I must get rid of her!' he thought savagely.

He was not certain how he could do so, however, without causing a scandal.

Irene might be improper.

She might, and most certainly did, shock a great number of older people in India.

At the same time, she was the daughter of a Duke, and the English are traditionally snobby.

Much that she did would be ignored and soon forgotten.

Somebody of less importance would immediately be ostracised.

"What can I do? What the devil can I do?" he asked himself a thousand times.

Because he found it impossible to sleep, he got out of bed and walked to the window.

There was not the faintest stirring of a breeze, and the atmosphere was heavy.

It was quite difficult to breathe.

As he stood by the window he heard a movement outside his door.

With a start he realised that incredibly, because he had not gone to Irene as she wanted, she was coming to him.

Undoubtedly she had found out—and she would not have had any scruples about how she did so—where he slept.

She would also know that he slept alone.

Lady Irene had not lived a life of intrigue without being able to discover anything she wished to know.

Lord Roydon had never imagined, however, that she would ignore all the rules of Social behaviour.

He was a married man sleeping next door to his wife.

How dare Irene come to his bed.

He was, however, used to being in dangerous situations.

His instinct invariably provided him with a way of escape.

Without a moment's hesitation he moved swiftly and opened the communicating-door between his room and Geta's.

He had expected she would be asleep.

Instead, her candles were still alight and she looked at him in surprise.

Softly shutting the door behind him, he walked across the room towards her bed.

Because he had got straight out of bed feeling very hot, he was wearing only a loin-cloth.

It was wound round his thighs, and his chest was bare.

Geta had never seen a man so naked before.

And yet, for the moment she did not think of Lord Roydon as a man.

Rather, because of his broad shoulders and his slim, athletic body, he reminded her of a Greek statue.

Her Father had been so proud of owning two.

Lord Roydon reached the bed and sat down on the side of it.

He thought, as he did so, that his wife was looking very lovely.

Her body was covered only by a sheet, and her nightgown was the thinnest she possessed.

It was easy to see the soft curves of her breasts.

He thought, as he had before, that she looked like a sprite from the woods.

For a moment neither of them spoke.

Then Lord Roydon said:

"I have come to ask you a question, Geta."

"A . . . question?"

"I thought this evening that it was not only too hot, but that there were too many people at dinner, and the atmosphere was not as amicable as I would have liked."

Geta knew exactly what he was saying.

He was apologising for Lady Irene's rudeness.

"What I am wondering," Lord Roydon went on, "is should we run away?"

Geta's eyes widened.

"Run away?" she repeated.

"We are going to Naini Tal anyway," he said, "but why not at once? Why not tomorrow morning, before all our guests are awake?"

"Could we . . . really do that?" Geta asked.

"Am I, or am I not, the Governor of the North-Western Provinces?" Lord Roydon asked. "And am I not, as Governor, able to make decisions which no-one may query?"

Geta clasped her hands together and laughed.

"Oh, please, Silvius, let us run away . . . to Naini Tal! It would be . . . very exciting!"

"Then that is what we will do," Lord Roydon said. "Can you be ready soon after dawn, which I think is soon after five o'clock?"

"Of course."

He smiled at her.

"Then I will put the wheels in motion and no-one will know that we have gone, or where we have gone. We will just have vanished!

"It is the most . . . exciting thing I have . . . ever heard!" Geta said. "I cannot tell you how . . . much I am looking . . . forward to seeing . . . the Himalayas."

It passed through Lord Roydon's mind that she might have said:

" . . . how much I am longing to be alone with you."

He rose from the bed before he said:

"They will be waiting—for both of us, and the

117

sooner we reach them, the better!"

"Thank you . . . oh . . . thank you for thinking of anything so . . . thrilling! Now I will go . . . to sleep because I want the morning to . . . come quickly."

Lord Roydon smiled at her before he walked across the room to the communicating-door.

He was aware as he did so that if Irene had come to his bedroom, as he was sure she had, she would have left when she found his bed empty.

He looked back at Geta.

She was sitting up in bed, her hands clasped together, her eyes shining with anticipation.

He wanted, as he had never wanted anything before, to take her in his arms.

He wanted to kiss her.

He wanted to tell her how lovely she was.

Then he told himself it was too soon.

She was excited by the thought of going to Naini Tal, not because she would be with him, but because she would see the Himalayas.

He stood for a long moment, just looking at her.

Then he went to his own room, shutting the door behind him.

chapter six

BECAUSE she was excited, Geta found it impossible to sleep.

She lay awake in the darkness.

She thought of how thrilling it would be to
escape from all the pomp and ceremony of Government House.

At first it had seemed like a fairy-tale with the
Army of servants in their red and white livery
and sentries on the door.

She and Silvius were accompanied everywhere
by *Aides-de-Camp*, until all she wanted was to be
alone with her husband.

As Governor, he seemed hardly to have a minute to himself.

She had to be content with catching sight of
him as he walked to the end of the corridor to
greet yet another deputation.

'In Naini Tal we will be able to talk,' she

thought confidently, 'and perhaps one day he will eventually tell me how unhappy he was as a little boy and I will be able to comfort him.'

She found herself haunted by the story of Silvius's suffering at the hands of his Step-mother.

She herself had been so happy as a child.

She knew that if she had children, they would know the same love her Mother had given to her and her two sisters.

"Another thing," Geta said to herself in the darkness, "is that Silvius will be safer at Naini Tal. Whatever danger is lurking here will vanish once we have gone away."

Dawn was just beginning to break when she jumped out of bed and started to dress.

She was arranging her hair when there was a knock on the door.

Kumar came in to call her.

"Lord *Sahib* gone downstairs, Lady *Sahib*," he said, "but no hurry. I pack everything while you breakfast."

Geta had not thought until now of the clothes she must take with her.

She was just about to give Kumar instructions, when she knew it would be a waste of time.

He would pack what he felt was necessary.

She was certain it would be exactly what she needed.

She finished arranging her hair, hardly looking in the mirror.

Picking up her hat and carrying it in her hand, she ran down the stairs.

She was not surprised to find the hall busy

with people running about, obviously obeying Silvius's instructions.

The Adjutant was organising everything.

The *Aides-de-Camp*, still half-asleep, were in attendance.

Servants hurried to and fro.

Geta went into the Breakfast-Room.

Everything had been set out as if they were breakfasting at their usual hour rather than two hours earlier.

She thought with a smile that with English servants it would have been impossible.

But the Indians were used to emergencies.

She had just seated herself, when Silvius came into the room.

"Good morning! You are delightfully punctual for a woman!" he exclaimed.

"I was so afraid that something at the last minute would prevent us from leaving," Geta answered.

"Everyone is obeying my orders," he said with satisfaction, "and I cannot think why you should have doubted it."

"I did not," she replied, "and I am lost in admiration that anything can be organised so skilfully. I was only afraid there might be an earthquake or a revolution to stop us from reaching the train."

"It will be waiting," Silvius said reassuringly, "and so will the Himalayas."

He smiled at her as he spoke.

She thought, although it might, of course, be her imagination, that he looked younger than he usually did.

Like herself, he was excited at escaping.

They left the Breakfast-Room and went to where the carriage was waiting for them.

Geta was not surprised to see another carriage behind it piled with their luggage and carrying both Kumar and Janar.

They had a Cavalry escort to take them to the station.

As they drove away, Geta did not dare look up at the windows.

She was afraid Lady Irene would be watching them.

At the station the Governor's Train was waiting.

There was the usual number of railway officials and *Aides-de-Camp* to see them off.

As the train began to move out of the station, their escort of soldiers stood at the salute.

"We have done it! We have done it!" Geta cried. "We have got away and I never really thought it would happen."

"Yes, we have done it," Silvius said with a note of triumph in his voice, "but there is a long journey ahead, so I suggest you make yourself comfortable."

Geta took off her hat and ran her fingers lightly through her hair.

She sat at the window and had a last look at Lucknow.

Silvius did not speak, and after a moment she turned to find him looking at her.

"Now, at last," she said, "I can ask you all the questions that have been running around in my head ever since we arrived in Lucknow."

"You know I would have answered them—if I could," Silvius replied.

Geta laughed.

"It was impossible to get near you! I could never have imagined a man so hemmed in until all I could see was just the top of his head!"

She was teasing him and his eyes were twinkling.

"Now," he replied, "we are isolated in this rather dilapidated Drawing-Room for enough hours for you to ask me questions about everything in the *Encyclopaedia Britannica!*"

"That is exactly what I intend to do," Geta replied. "But why dilapidated?"

She looked round the Drawing-Room as she spoke.

She realised it did, in fact, need redecorating, despite the fact that it was comfortable.

Silvius followed the direction of her eyes.

"I heard before I came North," he said, "that the Governor's Train was in bad shape. As soon as I think we can afford it, we will have a new one, and I promise you, it will be much faster than this!"

Their train was certainly very slow.

When they began to climb, it seemed only to crawl along.

Geta was half-afraid they would never reach Naini Tal.

She did, however, learn a great deal that she had wanted to know about the place to which they were escaping so furtively.

Silvius told her that it was not until 1839 that the British had discovered a certain lake.

It was hidden among the wooded peaks of the foothills of the Himalayas.

"It took forty years," he said, "for the hill station of Naini Tal to become the summer capital of the North-Western Provinces."

He paused to add:

"The lake, it is believed by the Indians, grew out of a hole dug by the goddess Naini, who had forbidden the place to strangers."

"Do you mean it is dangerous?" Geta asked apprehensively.

"Not now," Silvius replied, "but there was a fearful landslide in 1880 which buried the Hotel, the Assembly Rooms, and Library, together with a great many people."

He made a gesture with his hands.

"Of course the Indians said it was the goddess's way of punishing those who had invaded her privacy."

"But it is . . . safe . . . today?" Geta asked insistently.

"One of my predecessors, Sir John Strachey, was not afraid of the goddess's anger when he built himself a large new Government House, which is situated well out of the course of the landslides."

"And that is where we are going?"

"Of course," Silvius said. "And I think when you see it, you will agree with me that it is one of the loveliest places in the world."

Despite his enthusiasm, Geta could not help a little twinge of fear.

Were they going from one danger to another?

Then she told herself that she was being foolish.

Whatever she did, she must not spoil Silvius's pleasure in going to Naini Tal.

It might be because he was running away from Lady Irene!

She guessed that was the reason for their leaving so secretly.

But from her point of view it was a godsend.

To have her husband to herself she was prepared to brave the wrath of the goddess and danger from the Russians.

They talked, ate the food which the servants prepared for them on the train, and slept a little.

Finally, late in the evening the train chugged slowly into the station of Naini Tal.

A number of officials were waiting to greet Silvius.

Geta was relieved to see there was a large contingent of soldiers who had travelled on the train with them.

The station was in the valley.

There were carriages waiting to carry them up the long ascent to where Sir John Strachey had built his new Government House.

"It is 1,200 feet above the lake on a lofty peak and remote from Naini Tal," Silvius said, "just as Naini Tal is remote from India."

The horses drawing them began the long climb.

Geta looked ahead for her first glimpse of the Himalayas.

When it came, without even thinking what

she was doing, she reached out to take hold of Silvius's hand.

His fingers closed over hers.

He looked at her in surprise and found she was absorbed in looking ahead.

She could see the peaks of the Himalayas rising above the trees in the valley.

He saw the excitement on her face.

He did not speak but waited until she said in a rapt voice:

"How could . . . anything be . . . so beautiful?"

"That is what I think myself," he said quietly. "Every time I come here they mean more to me, and I know they have a message for all those who will listen."

Geta glanced at him in sheer surprise.

It was something she had never expected him to say.

Yet she already felt herself as if the dazzling white peaks were speaking to her.

It took a long time to climb higher and higher.

When at last she could see the rather unusual Government House, it looked to her not unlike a Scottish Castle.

Sir John had used yellow-grey stonework with which to build a long, two-storey mansion crowned with a number of battlemented turrets.

Some of the turrets were square, others octagonal.

He had added several verandahs and a complex of roofs.

It was certainly a house more suited to Scotland than to India.

And yet, with the Himalayas in the background and surrounded by trees, it had an attraction all its own.

By the time they reached the front-door where the sentries presented arms, it was growing dark.

The *Aides-de-Camp* were already in residence and greeted them.

On Silvius's orders they proceeded immediately to their private apartments.

Geta found that her room, which was large and comfortable, was next to Silvius's.

There was a private Sitting-Room opening out of hers.

As she stood looking round her, Silvius said quietly:

"I am arranging for us to dine in your Sitting-Room, so put on something loose and comfortable. There will be no guests—thank Heavens—tonight."

She smiled at him and thought as he moved away to his own room it was exactly what she would enjoy.

She had enormously admired the way huge dinners were staged in Lucknow.

The long table with its damask cloth, its display of glittering plate and crystal, was very impressive.

The napkins, cunningly folded to resemble fans or exotic birds, were, she learnt, traditional in the Lucknow Government House.

So were the *khitmutgars* in white, scarlet, and gold, one behind the chair of each guest.

As the Governor entered the Drawing-Room,

they were drawn up in line to salute him.

It was all fascinating to Geta, and she learnt that it was one of the many customs in the various Government Houses in the North-Western Provinces.

"In fact," the Adjutant told her, "there are more ceremonies observed here than in any of the other Provincial Houses apart from those used by the Viceroy."

It was therefore both a relief and an excitement when she went from her bedroom into the Sitting-Room.

She found a round table had been set for two, lit with candles, and decorated with flowers.

She had enjoyed a bath and rather shyly had put on, as Silvius had suggested, a negligee which had belonged to her Mother.

It was very pretty, trimmed with lace and velvet bows.

She wore only a nightgown beneath it instead of her corset.

Silvius was wearing a smoking-jacket of dark blue velvet which she had not seen before.

It was certainly a change from the evening-clothes laden with decorations which he habitually had worn in Lucknow.

As she crossed the room to reach him, he held out a glass of champagne, saying:

"A special treat in which we celebrate our escape to Naini Tal!"

Geta was surprised as she accepted the glass from him.

She knew how difficult it was, because of the heat, to keep and serve good wine in India.

As she took a sip of it, she said:

"I still find it hard to believe that we really have escaped!"

"You will believe it tomorrow, when I show you the view of the Himalayas from the garden," Silvius replied, "and there will be no deputations, no long-drawn-out meetings, and no decisions for the Governor to make."

"I am dreaming!" Geta exclaimed. "I know I am!"

Servants brought them food which she thought was particularly delicious.

They sat at the table talking for a long time.

There seemed so much to say, so much to talk about, so many subjects which Geta had never before discussed with anyone except her Father.

When at last they moved, the servants lifted up the table and took it out of the room.

"What I am going to show you now," Silvius said, "are some drawings that have been made by various visitors to Naini Tal. Some of them are really very clever."

He went to the bookcase and started looking amongst the shelves for the books he wanted.

It took a little time because he wished Geta to see only the best of the drawings, of which there was a large collection.

He found at last what he was seeking.

Then, as he turned round to take it to Geta, he saw that she had fallen asleep.

She had sat down on the sofa after dinner.

He had been talking to her while he searched the shelves, but had not realised that for a while she had not answered him.

Now he put down the book and, reaching the sofa, stood looking down at her.

She had rested her head against a cushion and had been sitting sideways until she put her legs up.

She was sound asleep.

Her eye-lashes were dark against the whiteness of her skin.

Silvius stood looking at her for a long time.

Then very gently he picked her up in his arms.

She did not wake, but only turned her face against his shoulder as if she were a child.

He carried her across the room and into her bedroom.

Kumar had left everything ready.

Silvius laid Geta's head down on the pillow before carefully removing her slippers.

He hesitated.

Slowly and carefully he undid the front of her negligee and slipped it from her arms.

She did not wake.

He tried not to think of how beautiful her body was through the transparency of her nightgown.

He covered her with the sheet and stood still, looking at her.

She was lovely—lovelier than any woman he had ever seen before.

Her beauty was different in every way from that of Irene and the other women he had known intimately.

How long he stood there he did not know.

Then at last he bent his head and very gently his lips touched hers.

He felt Geta give a little quiver, but she only turned her head to one side and went on sleeping.

Silvius blew out the candles and went to his own room.

* * *

The brilliance of the sunshine coming from the sides of the curtains told Geta that it was later than when she usually awoke.

She tried to remember what had happened last night.

Then she realised that she must have fallen asleep while Silvius was looking for the drawings.

"How could I have been so stupid and so discourteous as to go to sleep the very first time we were alone together?" she chided herself.

Then she remembered that they would be alone for some time at Naini Tal.

Nobody would know where they were.

"Are you quite certain," she had said to Silvius in the train, "that no-one will follow us?"

"The Adjutant will inform all enquirers that I have been called away on important business which is too secret to be talked about. We are travelling to a place which is forbidden to English travellers."

Geta laughed.

"Do you think they will believe him?"

"They have no alternative but to return to where they came from."

"And now we are alone at Naini Tal!" Geta

said to herself as she sat up in bed.

She rang the bell and a few minutes later Kumar appeared.

"Lady *Sahib* have good sleep," he said with satisfaction. "Lord *Sahib* say no hurry. He go buy horses, take Lady *Sahib* in garden when he return."

Geta thought the idea of Silvius buying horses an excellent one.

She was longing to ride with him.

He had told her there were plenty of places they could ride in Naini Tal.

She knew she would find them as fascinating as he did.

"I have so much to show you," he said, "and I do not think you will be bored."

Geta laughed.

"The word 'bored' does not apply to me, but I am afraid it may to you. Do you realise I have never seen you except surrounded by intelligent, important, fascinating, and, of course, beautiful people."

She thought of Lady Irene as she spoke.

She gave a little shudder.

"This is not only a voyage of escape," Silvius said, "but also one of discovery."

'We are discovering each other,' Geta thought now, 'and I do hope Silvius will not find me very dull.'

Once again she could see Lady Irene's beautiful face and glinting red hair.

She remembered the anger in her green eyes.

Then she thought that danger, for the moment at any rate, was past.

On Silvius's instructions her breakfast was brought to her in bed.

She learned that the eggs had come from a farm which provided Government House with milk, meat, and poultry.

It seemed to her very luxurious.

She remembered, too, that Silvius had told her there were many acres of forest and jungle inhabited by panthers and wild deer.

Because she felt she must see things for herself, as soon as she had finished her breakfast, Geta got up.

She wanted to go into the garden, but she knew it would be a mistake.

Silvius wanted to show it to her himself.

She had already been told how beautiful it was.

But she must wait until his return so that they could see it together.

She dressed, then decided to explore the house. But it was difficult not to keep going to the windows.

Just occasionally she caught a glimpse of the Himalayas through the branches.

It was then she had a sudden idea.

If she went up onto the roof, she would be able to see them far better than she could from inside the house or the garden.

Silvius had already explained to her the plan of the house.

The Drawing-Room was at the front and the Conservatory and a huge Ball-Room at the back.

It was not difficult to find a way up onto the roof.

She knew that in Indian houses in the very hot weather the men of the family would often sleep on the roof, where it would be cooler at night.

She found her way out onto the main part, then discovered a door leading into one of the battlemented turrets.

Inside, there was a twisting little staircase which took her to the top.

When she stepped out on the roof, she drew in her breath.

Just as she expected, the view of the Himalayas from here was fantastic!

Magnificent, dazzlingly white, they rose peak after peak behind and above each other.

She could understand that to the Indians they really were a world belonging to the gods upon which no-one might encroach.

She stood there for a long time.

She felt, as Silvius had said, as if they were speaking to her, telling her something of importance.

Just as she drew on her own Divine Power, so she felt she could draw on them.

Something spiritual and enlightening flowed from the peaks into her soul.

She was not exactly praying, but her whole being was lifted up.

She felt as if she were one with the gods and they spoke to her.

She stood there for such a long time that she thought perhaps Silvius might have returned and wonder where she was.

She was just about to turn away to go back

down the stairs when she looked down into the garden below her.

There were many trees, most of them in bloom.

They hid the flowers which she knew she would see later.

It was then she saw a movement.

She thought for a moment that it might be a deer, then was aware it was a man—a Holy Man—a *Saddhu*.

He was moving between the trees at the far end of the garden.

Because she had been caught up in the rapture of the Himalayas, she felt it was appropriate that the Holy Man should be there.

Then suddenly, and for no reason she could ascertain, she was afraid.

She knew that the Holy Men were respected everywhere in India.

No-one turned them away or prevented them from wandering where they wished.

And yet, where Silvius was concerned, could that not be a danger?

She told herself it was a ridiculous idea!

Still, some instinct within herself made her reason out that no-one else would be allowed into the garden now that Silvius was in residence.

But a Holy Man, because of everybody's respect for him, could go there unchallenged.

She looked down again, but the *Saddhu* could no longer be seen.

He could be anywhere, amongst the trees or seated beneath one.

No-one would dare to disturb him.

Geta looked again at the Himalayas.

Their dazzling whiteness told her nothing, only that inside herself she was secretly alarmed.

She turned and retraced her steps down the twisting stairway.

She reached the First Floor.

There was no-one in her Sitting-Room and she went on down to the Entrance Hall.

There was an *Aide-de-Camp* on duty, and through the open door Geta could see the sentries outside.

"Has His Excellency returned?" she asked the *Aide-de-Camp*.

"Not yet, Your Excellency," the young man replied, "but he should not be long."

Geta suddenly had an idea.

"I wonder if I could have a revolver?" she asked in a low voice.

The *Aide-de-Camp* looked surprised.

"To tell the truth," Geta said, "although I am rather ashamed to admit it, I am afraid of snakes."

The *Aide-de-Camp* smiled.

"Actually, Your Excellency, so am I, and I can find you a revolver, if you know how to use it."

"My Father taught me to handle one when I was quite young," Geta answered, "and I promise you, I will be very careful."

The *Aide-de-Camp* took her into a room which was beside the Governor's Study.

He opened a drawer and took out a revolver.

Geta knew it was the latest type.

It was small and not very heavy.

As she took it in her hand, she knew she would find it easy to handle if she had to do so.

The *Aide-de-Camp* gave her a small box of cartridges.

As she took them from him she said:

"I would rather you did not inform His Excellency that I have this revolver. He may think it cowardly of me to want it."

"I am sure he would not think that," the *Aide-de-Camp* replied, "but I will conveniently forget that Your Excellency has it in her possession."

"Thank you," Geta said as he smiled.

She slipped the revolver into the pocket of her full skirt.

Although she could feel it was against her leg, no-one would have the slightest idea that she was carrying a weapon of any sort.

As they walked back into the Hall, she heard a carriage draw up outside the front-door.

She heard the sentries present arms, and Silvius came hurrying through the doorway.

"Oh, here you are!" he exclaimed. "I have some good news for you—excellent news!"

Geta waited, her face turned up to his.

"I have bought four sprightly young horses," he said, "and they are all four in need of exercise!"

"How clever of you," Geta exclaimed, "and it will be marvellous to be able to ride again!"

"I remember what a good rider your Father was," Silvius remarked as they walked into the Drawing-Room. "I feel sure his daughter will be able to emulate him."

"I have ridden ever since I left the cradle," Geta replied, and they both laughed.

"The horses are arriving this afternoon," Silvius said, "and we will have our first ride tomorrow morning before it gets too hot."

"I cannot tell you how much I am looking forward to it," Geta replied.

"Just as I am," Silvius said quietly.

Their eyes met, and it was difficult for either of them to look away.

When she did so, Geta felt a strange feeling.

It was almost like a shaft of sunshine moving through her breast.

It was something she thought she had experienced before.

Then she knew it had happened last night in her dreams and she had forgotten about it until now.

There had been that strange, rapturous little feeling which made her feel shy.

"Perhaps I am imagining it," she told herself.

"Now I am going to tell you all about the horse . . ." Silvius was saying.

chapter seven

LUNCHEON was in the big Dining-Room.

It was rather Gothic in style, but Geta noticed at once that the open fireplace which in the Winter burnt logs was filled with flowers.

There were also flowers on the tables and flowers in huge vases in the corners of the room.

She thought it was what she would enjoy in any Dining-Room, and looked round her with delight.

Luncheon was delicious.

There was fresh trout from the mountain streams, young chickens from the farm, and a variety of fruits from the garden.

Silvius drank only fruit-juice.

Like most sensible Englishmen in India, he made it a rule never to drink alcohol before the sun went down.

He had so much to tell Geta about the horses that it was difficult to concentrate on anything else.

They had belonged to an elderly soldier who was an outstanding Polo Player.

He was leaving India and going home.

"The Colonel has two more superb horses," Silvius was saying, "but he is thinking of taking them with him. I feel, however, that if you and I went to see him tomorrow, we might persuade him to let us have those as well."

"Oh, do let us try!" Geta said.

Then she added with a sigh:

"Except, of course, I feel sorry for the poor man having to leave behind the animals he loves."

"He will find plenty more to suit him in England," Silvius said, "but it is not so easy in India to find really good horses. The Army is rather hard on them."

Geta was sure this was true, especially where they were now, near the North-West Frontier.

When they had finished their coffee, Silvius rose to his feet.

"And now," he said, "I am going to show you what I think is the most beautiful garden in the whole world!"

He went to the door and opened it. As Geta reached it, he said:

"I am glad you are wearing a green gown. You will look as if you are part of the garden."

She was pleased that he had noticed what she was wearing.

She must, she thought, have put on her simple

green muslin gown today instinctively.

The sun was shining brightly.

But the heat was not stifling high up where they were amongst the mountains as it would have been down in the Plains.

Geta could think only with pity of those who had to endure the long Summer.

However, usually the wives of the soldiers could escape to Simla.

As they walked into the Hall, an *Aide-de-Camp* rose hastily to his feet.

The sentries presented arms as they went out through the front-door.

Geta had, of course, seen the front of the house when she first arrived.

Now Silvius took her round to the side, and instantly she was in the garden itself.

The first thing she noticed was the fragrance of Lilies-of-the-Valley.

When she looked she saw a profusion of them, white and graceful, growing apparently wild amongst the grass.

"How lovely!" she exclaimed.

"Wait," he warned, "or you will run out of adjectives."

They went on a little farther.

There were rhododendron bushes—scarlet, pink, and white—vivid against the trees that were also in blossom.

It was then that Geta saw that the paths along which they were walking were lined with mauve orchids just coming into bud.

It was something she had never expected or even imagined before.

She stood entranced at the sight of them until Silvius laughed.

"I knew you would be surprised," he said.

"They are lovely—lovely!" Geta cried.

He pointed out the white Clematis that covered the jungle shrubs until they seemed almost to rival the snow on the mountains.

Because Geta was lingering over the orchids, Silvius put out his hand and took hers.

"We have still a long way to go," he said, "so you must stand and be hypnotised by the orchids another time!"

He laughed as he added:

"You can also calculate how expensive it would be if I had to buy each one for you to wear on your shoulder."

Geta laughed too.

Then he set off across the grass, moving away from the house until it was no longer in sight.

She wondered what Silvius intended to show her next.

Unexpectedly, as they moved amongst the trees, there was a clearing in front of them, and she could see the Himalayas.

The sunlight on them was dazzling.

Without her meaning to, her fingers tightened in Silvius's hand, and he was aware of how excited she was.

The path came to an abrupt end.

Geta realised they had reached a sheer drop of hundreds of feet, which was where the landslide had taken place.

The drop seemed fathomless and a faint cloud curled beneath them.

She could see at the sides there were rough, pointed rocks, but her eyes kept going to the mountains overhead.

Almost as if the gods were showing her the wonder of their possessions, a cloud before them moved slowly away.

It revealed the stupendous panorama of the Plains, stretching into the distance below them.

"It cannot be true!" Geta murmured.

"That is what I thought when I first came here," Silvius answered. "Now you can catch a glimpse of the lake where the Goddess Naini, who owned all this beauty, lived, and I am sure still does."

"Of course she does," Geta agreed.

They stood in silence.

Geta felt as if the Himalayas towering above them were speaking to her.

She longed to feel the presence of the goddess who owned the lake and was responsible for the beauty of the flowers.

It was Silvius who finally turned to take her back.

She wanted to ask him to let her stay there for hours.

Then she thought as he had seen it all before, perhaps he would be bored and so she said nothing.

They walked in silence.

There was only the song of the birds in the trees, the humming of the bees over the flowers, and an occasional scuffle amongst the undergrowth from some small animal.

Silvius was still holding her hand.

Geta thought it was like being in Paradise to walk beside him, to be alone and to know for the moment, at any rate, nobody could interrupt them.

They had moved away from the open path which ended with the great drop of the landslide.

Now there were once again the huge bushes of rhododendrons.

It was then suddenly that Geta's dreamlike feeling dissolved and she became aware of danger.

It was the same feeling she had had when she was on the roof.

It invaded her mind so strongly that she felt she must tell Silvius about it.

Then she thought he would merely think she was being hysterical.

They were safe in Naini Tal—far safer than they had been in Lucknow.

But the feeling persisted like an insistent intrusion in her mind.

Instinctively, because despite herself she was frightened, she slipped her right hand into the pocket of her skirt.

She clasped the small revolver.

She had forgotten about it while she was looking at the beauty they had seen at the landslide.

Now, because the revolver was heavy against her leg, she was vitally aware of it, also glad, although it seemed unnecessary, that it was there.

Silvius led her towards the rhododendrons.

He was just about to point out to Geta a new variety.

Suddenly from the bushes only a few feet away from them appeared the *Saddhu*.

He came out through the blossom, and Geta first saw his bare head.

So swiftly that it was like a flash of lightning, she was aware that he carried in his hand a long, sharp knife.

For one second his whole body was revealed.

Then he sprang at Silvius.

Without even thinking, Geta fired at him.

The bullet passed through the thin muslin of her gown, hitting the *Saddhu* in the stomach.

He staggered, and still without conscious thought Geta pulled the revolver out of her pocket.

She shot him again—this time in the heart.

He crashed backwards onto the ground.

Geta could only stand staring at him, the smoking revolver in her hand.

Silvius went into action.

He took the revolver from her and said in a quiet, calm voice:

"Go back to the house, my Darling. Go straight to your room and speak to nobody until I join you."

For a moment she found it hard to understand what he was saying.

She had killed a man!

Yet it did not seem possible it had happened.

The *Saddhu* was lying on the ground in front of her.

The long, sharp knife he had carried was lying a little way away from him on the grass.

Her ears were still ringing from the sound of the explosions.

But she had heard what Silvius said to her.

A second after, she heard voices in the distance and footsteps running towards them.

"Go!" Silvius said firmly.

It was an order.

Geta gave him a startled glance before swiftly she slipped away through the bushes.

Knowing she must obey Silvius, she ran along the twisting paths that led her to the house.

Only as she reached the gravelled carriageway did she force herself to walk with dignity past the sentries.

There was no *Aide-de-Camp* in the Hall.

She thought he must have gone with the soldiers when they had heard the revolver shots.

She ran up the stairs without being seen, entered her bedroom, and shut the door behind her.

For a moment she leant against it as if for support.

She had saved Silvius—saved him from being kiled by the *Saddhu*.

It was her Divine Power which had told her of the danger.

If she had not gone up onto the roof, if she had not seen the *Saddhu* and known that because he was a Holy Man nobody would interfere with him, she would not have asked for the revolver.

In which case, it would have been Silvius who was lying dead in the garden.

Perhaps she, too, would have been dead beside him.

Because she felt her legs would no longer hold her, she went down on her knees.

Putting her head against the mattress of her bed, she thanked God for saving Silvius.

She prayed for a long time.

When she rose to her feet she saw the hole in her gown through which the first bullet had passed.

Quickly she took it off.

She knew it was a gown she would never wear again.

It would always remind her that she had been responsible for the death of a man.

But Silvius was alive!

Her heart was singing because she had been able to save him.

After taking off her gown she felt cold and knew it was from shock.

She put on her nightgown and got into bed.

The sun-blinds had been lowered and the room was cool, dim, and very quiet.

She began to feel afraid.

Suppose there had been other assassins in the garden supporting the *Saddhu*.

Suppose before the soldiers could reach him Silvius was attacked again?

She wished now she had not obeyed him by running away.

Then she remembered!

Though he had taken the revolver from her, the remaining bullets were still in the pocket of her gown.

She sat up in bed because she wanted to go back to join him.

Then she remembered how firmly he had ordered her to go back to the house.

He had seemed quiet and calm, and completely in control of the situation.

Besides, the soldiers would be with him by now.

The *Aide-de-Camp* could call for more troops if they were wanted.

She knew the soldiers who guarded Silvius were specially picked men who had come with them from Lucknow.

'They should have been watching over him!' she thought angrily. 'They should not have allowed him to go into the garden alone with me without a guard.'

Then she was sure that it would have been Silvius's orders that they should not be disturbed.

How could he have thought . . . how could he have imagined for a moment that a *Saddhu*, who is sacred to the Indians, could really be one of his enemies in disguise?

No real Holy Man would take life.

It was, Geta had to admit, clever of his enemies to have thought of such an original way of approaching him.

"But he is safe . . . because I . . . saved him!" she told herself.

It was something she repeated a hundred times.

At last she realised that a long time had elapsed since she had left Silvius.

He had not come to her.

By now the sun had lost most of its strength.

Because she was frightened to the point where she could not keep still, Geta jumped out of bed.

She went to the window and pulled up the sun-blind.

Now she could see the trees below her in the garden.

Far away in the distance there was a brilliant light which still enveloped the tops of the mountains.

They had told her how to save Silvius.

But he had not yet returned, and perhaps something terrible had happened to him.

He had told her to speak to no-one.

Now she had to force herself not to ring the bell, not to go to the door and ask any servant who was within ear-shot where the Lord *Sahib* was.

She walked across the room.

Yet, when she reached the door she felt she could hear his voice saying:

"Speak to nobody."

She went back to the window.

"Save him! Oh, God, save him!" she murmured.

How could he be so long? What had happened to him?

Why had he not come?

The questions seemed almost to be shouted aloud in the empty room.

Then when she felt she must scream because she was so afraid, the door opened.

Silvius was there.

He came in and shut the door behind him.

He stood looking at her, and for a moment Geta could not move.

Then with a cry that came from the very depths of her heart she ran towards him and flung herself against him.

His arms went round her and his lips came down on hers.

Then he was kissing her, kissing her wildly, passionately, demandingly.

It was as if, like her, he had waited an eternity and had reached breaking-point.

He kissed Geta until she felt as if he lifted her from the valley of darkness into the light of the mountains.

He kissed her until she could no longer think, but only feel.

It was then he slipped her nightgown down from her shoulders.

Lifting her in his arms, he carried her to the bed and laid her down on it.

She was so bemused and enraptured by his kisses that Geta could only lie where he had put her.

She looked blindly at the light coming through the window.

Then Silvius was beside her, drawing her close to him.

She felt the hardness of his body against the softness of her own, and it was as if she melted into him.

She was no longer herself, but his.

He kissed her eyes, her lips, the softness of her neck, and her breasts.

The sunshine that had seemed to quiver within her now turned into flame.

She felt it was part of the fire that burned in Silvius.

It carried them both up to the peaks of ecstasy, where there were only the gods, and they were one with them.

* * *

A long time later Geta whispered against Silvius's shoulder:

"I . . . I love . . . you!"

They were the first words either of them had spoken since he had come into the room.

And yet she felt they had said a thousand things to each other which they both understood.

Silvius's arms tightened.

"My Precious, my wonderful, perfect little wife!" he said. "I have not hurt you?"

"We reached the peaks of the Himalayas," Geta answered, "and . . . I have . . . never known . . . anything so . . . wonderful!"

"I thought the same," Silvius said, "and, my Precious, my Darling, I must thank you for saving my life!"

Geta put her hand on his chest, as if she would protect him.

"Will there . . . be other . . . men?" she murmured in a frightened tone.

Silvius shook his head.

"No," he said, "that particular danger is over."

Geta was still.

"Do you mean . . . there were . . . other *Saddhus*?"

"Two more," Silvius replied, "but they will not trouble us again."

Geta knew that was what had worried her.

"Oh, Darling, are you . . . sure?" she murmured.

"You know that is something I cannot talk about," Silvius said. "The whole episode is finished. Their mission, if that is what it was, has failed."

"But the Russians may . . . try again," Geta said in a frightened voice.

"Not in that particular way nor, I think, in this particular place," Silvius said. "Besides, they will not know for a long time what a failure their effort has been."

Geta knew without his saying so that they must have found and put to death the two other men.

They and the *Saddhu* whom she had shot would have been buried secretly.

Nobody else would be aware of it, except for the soldiers concerned.

"You must not think about it any more," Silvius said, "but I do want to tell you, my Darling, how brave and marvellous you were."

He paused before he added:

"I learnt how it was you were carrying a revolver, and it was very clever of you to obtain it in such a simple manner."

Geta moved a little nearer to him.

"It was the . . . gods of the Himalayas . . . who told me of . . . the danger," she said in a hesitating little voice.

"Why did you not tell me?" Silvius asked.

"I was afraid you might think I was being . . . over-imaginative—perhaps even hysterical."

"That is something I will never do—I believe in your Divine Power, and because of it we will be very happy together."

He drew her a little closer before he asked:

"I have made you happy? You do love me?"

"I love you . . . I love . . . you," Geta said.

There was a little pause, then Silvius said slowly:

"I am going to say to you what, I swear before God, I have never said to any other woman before: I love you, my brave and beautiful wife!"

Because of the sincerity with which he spoke, Geta felt the tears come into her eyes.

"Oh, Darling," she said, "that is a wonderful thing to tell me . . . and I love you."

"As I love you," Silvius answered, "with my body, my heart, and my soul. This is what you wanted?"

"Everything I wanted!" Geta cried. "And I promise that I will try to make you happy so that never again will you be miserable . . . or hurt by . . . anyone."

She was thinking not so much of his assailants as of his Stepmother.

As if he understood, but had no words in which to reply, Silvius sought her lips.

He kissed her, and first it was a kiss of dedication.

Then, as if the softness and sweetness of her was irresistible, his kiss became more passionate.

Once again the flames were moving within Geta's breast, and they were flying side by side up towards the peaks of ecstasy.

* * *

"Is this really our last night?" Geta asked.

She turned from the window as she spoke.

She had been looking up at the stars coming out like a profusion of diamonds in the darkness of the sky.

"The last night of our honeymoon," Silvius replied. "Tomorrow we start our married life as a respectable married couple who have become used to each other!"

Geta laughed and ran across the room to where he was sitting on the sofa.

It was their last night before Silvius admitted he was the Governor in residence and was ready to receive deputations.

He was prepared now to start the work that awaited him.

They therefore dined, as they had done the first night they arrived, in Geta's private Sitting-Room.

The table, decorated with mauve orchids, had been carried from the room.

Now they were alone.

Geta sat down beside Silvius and asked:

"Do you really think we will ever be prosaic and respectable and become bored with each other?"

She was speaking in the same mocking way that he had.

At the same time, Silvius was aware that there was a frightened look in her eyes.

He put his arm around her and drew her close to him before he answered:

"We came here on a voyage of discovery, and I still have a great deal to discover about the strange, unusual, enigmatic young woman I can now call my wife."

"I hope I am all of those things," Geta said, "but you forgot to add how much I love you."

"I thought you would tell me about that," Silvius said.

"I love you! I love you!" Geta replied. "Every day I think it impossible to love you more than I do already, and yet the next morning I know I love you a million times more!"

"That is what I feel about you," Silvius said as he smiled. "You intrigue, bewitch, and excite me."

"As you excite me!" Geta murmured.

He pulled her a little closer and would have kissed her, but she put up her hand.

"I have something exciting to tell you which I have kept for tonight as a surprise."

"You have been keeping something from me?" he asked. "You know you are not allowed to do that! I want to know everything that is in your mind, and I am jealous of anything you think of besides me. I certainly resent any secrets you withhold from me!"

"But this is a present which I wanted to give you tonight so that it would be not only a . . . sad occasion because our honeymoon is over . . . but also a happy one."

"We will have a hundred other honeymoons," Silvius said, "and each one of them will be more exciting and more thrilling, my Darling, than the last."

"That is a promise which I will make you keep," Geta replied, "but try to be interested in my present to you."

"I am interested," Silvius said, "but as usual, when I look at you I become excited and can think of nothing but that I want you closer to me than you are at this moment."

Geta felt a thrill run through her because she knew that what he was saying was the truth.

She put her fingers on his lips to prevent him from kissing her and begged:

"Please, Darling, listen."

"I am listening," Silvius said, "but do not be long about it!"

She could see the passion in his eyes and knew it was the most wonderful thing that could ever happen to her.

But she managed to say quietly:

"I received a letter yesterday from Madeline. She told me something very exciting. The Cousin to whom my Father left our house has been killed in a railway accident in Spain."

She saw Silvius look surprised.

"You do remember that Papa left him Wick House, which was something we all resented?"

"Then what happens now?" Silvius asked.

"Madeline has been in touch with Linette, and they have agreed that because their husbands have their own ancestral homes, Wick House should be mine," Geta replied.

She saw the surprise in Silvius's eyes, and went on:

"Do you not see, my Darling, it is a perfect idea? It is already a part of your title, and it will be our home . . . a home where we can go when you have the time, when you retire, and there . . ."

She paused and blushed before hiding her face against him, and she whispered:

" . . . we can . . . bring up . . . our . . . children."

"And they will be happy," Silvius said.

"Very, very happy," Geta agreed, "and they will never, my Darling, Wonderful husband, be miserable, as you were, in a house that will be full of love because . . . we love each other . . . so much."

She looked up at him as she spoke.

Then Silvius's lips were on hers.

She felt the fire within him.

She knew that not only did he want her as he had already said he did, but what she had told him had also excited him.

She had known when she had read her sister's letter that nothing could be more perfect.

The beautiful Queen Anne house which her Father and Mother had made so attractive could be a home for her and Silvius.

It would be a home where they could have their children and their horses.

It would be filled with all the happiness Silvius had never known after his Mother had died.

She knew without Silvius saying so that the same thoughts were running through his mind.

But he kissed her and went on kissing her.

Then there was no need for words as he felt the fire burning in him moving like little flames from Geta's breasts onto her lips.

He lifted her up and carried her through the communicating-door into her bedroom.

The candles had not been lit and the curtains were drawn back.

The moonlight was shining like a silver stream to sweep away the darkness.

As Silvius made Geta his, he carried her up to the peaks of the Himalayas, where the moonlight enveloped them in all its glory.

Their love was not human, but Divine and would go on unto Eternity.

ABOUT THE AUTHOR

Barbara Cartland, the world's most famous romantic novelist, who is also an historian, playwright, lecturer, political speaker and television personality, has now written over 570 books and sold over six hundred and twenty million copies all over the world.

She has also had many historical works published and has written four autobiographies as well as the biographies of her mother and that of her brother, Ronald Cartland, who was the first Member of Parliament to be killed in the last war. This book has a preface by Sir Winston Churchill and has just been republished with an introduction by Sir Arthur Bryant.

Love at the Helm, a novel written with the help and inspiration of the late Earl Mountbatten of Burma, Great Uncle of His Royal Highness, The Prince of Wales, is being sold for the Mountbatten Memorial Trust.

She has broken the world record for the last sixteen years by writing an average of twenty-three books a year. In the *Guinness Book of World Records* she is listed as the world's top-selling author.

Miss Cartland in 1987 sang an Album of Love Songs with the Royal Philharmonic Orchestra.

In private life Barbara Cartland, who is a Dame of the Order of St. John of Jerusalem, Chairman of the St. John Council in Hertfordshire and Deputy President of the St. John Ambulance Brigade, has fought for better conditions and salaries for Mid-wives and Nurses.

She championed the cause for the Elderly in 1956 invoking a Government Enquiry into the "Housing Condition of Old People."

In 1962 she had the Law of England changed so that Local Authorities had to provide camps for their own Gypsies. This has meant that since then thousands and thousands of Gypsy children have been able to go to School, which they had never been able to do in the past, as their caravans were moved every twenty-four hours by the Police.

There are now fourteen camps in Hertfordshire and Barbara Cartland has her own Romany Gypsy Camp called Barbaraville by the Gypsies.

Her designs "Decorating with Love" are being sold all over the U.S.A. and the National Home Fashions League made her, in 1981, "Woman of Achievement."

She is unique in that she was one and two in the Dalton list of Best Sellers, and one week had four books in the top twenty.

Barbara Cartland's book *Getting Older, Growing Younger* has been published in Great Britain and the U.S.A. and her fifth cookery book, *The Romance of Food*, is now being used by the House of Commons.

In 1984 she received at Kennedy Airport America's Bishop Wright Air Industry Award for her contribution to the development of aviation. In 1931 she and two R.A.F. Officers thought of, and carried, the first aeroplane-towed glider airmail.

During the War she was Chief Lady Welfare Officer in Bedfordshire, looking after 20,000 Servicemen and -women. She thought of having a pool of Wedding Dresses at the War Office so a Service Bride could hire a gown for the day.

She bought 1,000 gowns without coupons for the A.T.S., the W.A.A.F.'s and the W.R.E.N.S. In 1945 Barbara Cartland received the Certificate of Merit from Eastern Command.

In 1964 Barbara Cartland founded the National Association for Health of which she is the President, as a front for all the Health Stores and for any product made as alternative medicine.

This is now a £65 million turnover a year, with one-third going in export.

In January 1968 she received *La Médeille de Vermeil de la Ville de Paris*. This is the highest award to be given in France by the City of Paris. She has sold 25 million books in France.

Barbara Cartland was received with great enthusiasm by her fans, who feted her at a reception in the City, and she received the gift of an embossed plate from the Government.

In March 1988 Barbara Cartland was asked by the Indian Government to open their Health Resort outside Delhi. This is almost the largest Health Resort in the world.

Barbara Cartland was made a Dame of the Order of the British Empire in the 1991 New Year's Honours List by Her Majesty, The Queen, for her contribution to Literature and also for her years of work for the community.

Dame Barbara has now written the greatest number of books by a British author passing the 564 books written by John Creasey.

AWARDS

1945   Received Certificate of Merit, Eastern Command, for being Welfare Officer to 5,000 troops in Bedfordshire.

1953   Made a Commander of the Order of St. John of Jerusalem. Invested by H.R.H. The Duke of Gloucester at Buckingham Palace.

1972   Invested as Dame of Grace of the Order of St. John in London by The Lord Prior, Lord Cacia.

1981   Received "Achiever of the Year" from the National Home Furnishing Association in Colorado Springs, U.S.A., for her designs for wallpaper and fabrics.

1984   Received Bishop Wright Air Industry Award at Kennedy Airport, for inventing the aeroplane-towed glider.

1988   Received from Monsieur Chirac, The Prime Minister, The Gold Medal of the City of Paris, at the Hotel de la Ville, Paris, for selling 25 million books and giving a lot of employment.

1991   Invested as Dame of the Order of The British Empire, by H.M. The Queen at Buckingham Palace for her contribution to Literature.

Called after her own beloved Camfield Place, each Camfield Novel of Love by Barbara Cartland is a thrilling, never-before published love story by the greatest romance writer of all time.

Barbara Cartland